DICKINSON AREA PUBLIC LIBRARY

3 3121 00144 2461

J F De la Cruz, M. B6581 V. 4.5
De la Cruz, Melissa.
Keys to the repository

(Blue Bloods #4.5)

AUG 26 '10

WITHDRAWN FROM
Dickinson Public Library

D0951940

Blue Bloods

⊷ KEYS TO THE REPOSITORY ⊷

Also by Melissa de la Cruz

Blue Bloods

⊶ KEYS TO THE REPOSITORY ⊷

MELISSA DE LA CRUZ

Illustrations by Michael Johnston

HYPERION
NEW YORK

DICKINSON AREA PUBLIC
LIBRARY
139 Third Street West
Dickinson, North Dakota 58601

Text and illustrations copyright © 2010 by Melissa de la Cruz
"Shelter Island" copyright © 2007 by Melissa de la Cruz, a version
of which first appeared in *666: The Number of the Beast*, published by Point,
an imprint of Scholastic Inc. Reprinted by permission of Scholastic Inc.

All rights reserved. Published by Hyperion,
an imprint of Disney Book Group. No part of this book may be
reproduced or transmitted in any form or by any means, electronic
or mechanical, including photocopying, recording, or by any
information storage and retrieval system, without written
permission from the publisher. For information address
Hyperion, 114 Fifth Avenue, New York, New York 10011-5690.

First Edition
10 9 8 7 6 5 4 3 2 1
V567-9638-5-10105
Printed in the United States of America
Designed by Elizabeth H. Clark

Library of Congress Cataloging-in-Publication Data on file.
ISBN 978-1-4231-3454-1
Reinforced binding

Visit www.bluebloodsbooks.com
Visit www.hyperionteens.com

For my family: Mike, Mattie, Mom, Aina, Steve, Nicholas, Joseph, Chit, and Christina, and the memory of Pop

CONTENTS

The possession of knowledge does not kill the sense of wonder and mystery. There is always more mystery.

—Anaïs Nin

Dear Constant Reader,

When I was growing up, I was a huge fan of Stephen King's books (I still am). And something I remember so vividly about reading his books is that once in a while he would include a letter to his readers in the introduction. These letters were addressed "Dear Constant Reader" because as he published more and more novels, it became apparent to him that his readers were eating them up—reading them as fast as he could write them, and so he wanted to thank them for that, and to celebrate it as well. In his letters he would give us a little insight into how he wrote his books, what inspired them, how they were written, and what he thought about them once finished.

I **loved** these letters. I think I secretly enjoyed his letters a little more than the books themselves. As someone who had read all of his books, I was fascinated by this glimpse into their inner workings, and to be told something more about the stories—a background history, an inspiration, a governing idea, maybe—that was not to be found in the pages themselves.

If you are holding this book in your hands, I hope it's safe for me to assume that you are *my* Constant Reader, and that you are curious to find out a little more about the world of the Blue Bloods beyond what has been available in the novels so far. And for that, I am extremely tickled, humbled, and gratified. It's always been a dream of mine to write a book like this, a companion book to the series. I absolutely adore companion books. On my shelf next to my many Stephen King novels, you will also find *The Dark Tower: A Concordance, Volume 1* and *The Road to the Dark Tower: Exploring Stephen King's Magnum Opus*.

I'd like to share a little bit about the Blue Bloods series—how I first imagined it and how it came to be and how the work is going. The story behind the story, so to speak. As King says, "Some people don't want to know how sausage is made; if so, skip this and go ahead to the real meal." So if you don't want to hear about the backstory, you don't have to read this. But if you do, here it is.

When my editor asked if I ever wanted to try

my hand at a horror/fantasy book, I responded with a resounding YES! YES! YES! As soon as I got off the phone with her, my mind was whirling with so many ideas. I knew from the beginning I wanted to write a big epic fantasy, like my favorite books from childhood: King's Dark Tower series, Isaac Asimov's The Foundation trilogy, J.R.R. Tolkien's The Lord of the Rings, Anne Rice's Vampire Chronicles. But I also wanted to set the story in the modern world, like J.K. Rowling's wonderful Harry Potter books, which reminded me, as an adult, how pleasurable reading books could be. I especially wanted to set it in New York City, my home, which I had just left and missed terribly, as we had moved to Los Angeles in late 2003.

It just happened that at the time my editor called, I was tooling around on the Internet and had found a Web site that listed every passenger on the *Mayflower*, along with their notable descendants. The list was the "lightning bulb" from the beginning: I thought, what if all these wealthy, important, and influential Americans (the list includes the likes of the Bushes and the Roosevelts, but also—which I thought was more interesting—American icons like Oprah and Marilyn

Monroe)—what if all these great people had come to be that way because they were . . . (da da dum . . .) UNDEAD? (BWAHA-HA-HA-HA.)

My other idea was that I very much wanted to have an origin story for my vampires. I had yet to come across a vampire novel that had one. I wanted a believable explanation for their existence. I had always loved the story of *Paradise Lost* and found Lucifer's fall incredibly romantic and tragic. And so: the *Mayflower*, the New York elite, and vampires as cursed angels who fell with Lucifer—my outline was really starting to take shape.

I imagined a large, sprawling story with a huge cast of characters. Some pieces came into place easily: three girls, three different motivations. Schuyler, the shy girl who might hold the key to the Blue Bloods' salvation; Mimi, whose superficial façade masks her true nature; and Bliss, who hides a dangerous secret. Other pieces, like how the Lost Colony of Roanoke figured into the tale, came as I was writing the first book. Soon I was off and running, and now, five years later, I am more immersed in the story than ever. It is alive in my mind, the Blue Bloods' saga dominates talk at my dinner table (my husband is a supportive sounding board), I spend my days turning over plot points, and I can't sleep if I can't solve a character's dilemma.

In these pages you'll find the mythology of the Blue Bloods explained, some new stories featuring our favorite young vampires, and a sneak peek at what's to come. I should warn you, The Repository Files, which include character profiles, were written by rather crotchety historians who work for the humorless Committee, so you might find their estimation of the characters a little astringent. Also, while the Repository might think they know everything, careful readers will observe that in certain instances their knowledge is somewhat limited.

Thank you for welcoming the Blue Bloods into your library. I have very much enjoyed the journey that has brought them to your shelves.

I don't remember how Stephen King said good-bye to his readers, but for me, it's always a very fond . . .

xoxo

Mel

THE REPOSITORY FILES

The following documents you are about to read contain top secret and classified information concerning the history of the Blue Bloods. These records were compiled and maintained by Conduit Renfield, the Repository's longest-serving historian, along with higher-ranking scribes and their interns. The Committee employs a secret underground network of Wardens, Venators, Conduits, and interns to keep their members safe and also to keep track of their actions and whereabouts. In Blue Bloods *(or Repository Record #101), Mimi Force said of the Committee Wardens: "It was eerie how they knew so much about you—almost as if they were always there, watching." She was right.*

ONCE UPON A TIME IN PARADISE
The Fall and Rise of the Blue Bloods

It was the beginning of the end. Lucifer, the Prince of Heaven, the Morningstar, the most beautiful angel of all time, became so enamored with his own beauty and power that he came to believe his light was as great as the Almighty, and that the throne should be his and his alone. And so he gathered his loyal army of angels for the War to End All Wars, and with swords blazing, trumpets blasting, and hellfire in his heart, he came to claim what was not his to claim.

The battle was a day of black smoke and searing flame, clashing swords and cracking whips. Alas, with victory in Lucifer's grasp, at the crucial moment to deliver the crushing blow, the twin Angels of the

Apocalypse—Abbadon and Azrael—his most loyal lieutenants, stayed their hand. They betrayed the Morningstar and knelt to the golden sword of Michael instead, turning the tide of battle. But it was too late to save themselves.

All the rogue angels were banished from Heaven. They woke to the cold of the earth as immortals, condemned to walk the world forever, and cursed until the end of days to feed on the blood of their human brethren. Where once they were angels, they were now "vampyres." Angels of fire and death. Soulless creatures bereft of light and love, with the immortal blue blood running in their veins.

But they were not without hope. Gabrielle, the Virtuous, out of love for her people, chose to descend with them, to bring a ray of light to the damned. She was joined by her mate, the mightiest of them all, Michael, Pure of Heart, who could not bear to spend eternity apart from her. Gabrielle and Michael were called the Uncorrupted, vampires by choice instead of sin.

Together, Gabrielle and Michael established the Code of the Vampires, a foundation of rules that would govern their community through the centuries, and help them to forge a way back to their glorious home in Paradise. The life cycles of the vampires were coordinated to match a human lifetime, and so the vampires followed the rites of life (Expression), death (Expulsion), and reincarnation (Evolution).

But Lucifer and his minions remained contemptuous of their fall from Paradise. They had no desire to regain God's grace or to live by the Code. They preyed on their fellow vampires, feeding on their blood and memories until they became beings of chaos, misery, and delirium. Their blood turned silver, and they were called Croatan, the Silver Bloods.

For a time they were subdued and controlled by the power of the Uncorrupted, and for centuries served as the Blue Bloods' slaves. That is, until the day the slaves rose up against their masters in a merciless slaughter. Thus did Michael declare war against Lucifer and his followers, seeking revenge and bringing death and havoc to his enemies.

The war culminated in a final battle in ancient Rome, when Cassius (Michael) unmasked the emperor Caligula, who was revealed to be Lucifer himself. Michael sent Lucifer into the fires of Hell by the point of his golden sword, forever locking him behind an impenetrable gate.

After Rome, for millennia the Blue Bloods lived in relative safety. However, every hundred years or so, rumors persisted of attacks on young vampires in Venice, Florence, Barcelona, and Cologne, but information was inconclusive, and later suppressed. For all intents and purposes, the community believed the Silver Bloods had been destroyed.

Distressed by the rise of religious persecution in Europe in the seventeenth century, a coven of Blue Bloods crossed to America, looking for peace. But the ancient evil followed them there, with a rash of mysterious disappearances at Plymouth. A few years later, their entire settlement at Roanoke was taken, with no clue as to their whereabouts except for a lone message— "Croatan"—nailed on a tree.

During this time of chaos in Plymouth, John Carver (the angel Metraton) called for a White Vote to challenge the leadership and gain the title of Regis of the Coven. John and his wife, Catherine Carver (the angel Seraphiel), were convinced that the Silver Bloods had never been fully vanquished and that a traitor Silver Blood was hidden among their ranks; that one of their own was Corrupted. John Carver agitated for vigilance and an investigation.

But Myles Standish (the archangel Michael) was equally passionate in his belief that the Silver Bloods no longer walked the earth. For the first time in Blue Blood history there was disagreement within the Conclave of Elders. But John Carver lost the White Vote, as the Conclave chose Myles Standish, thereby confirming their faith in Michael once again. The Carvers lost their governing position in the Conclave, their lone opposing voice silenced under the Regis's ironfisted rule.

As the years went by, the Blue Bloods grew comfortable, satisfied, fearless, and proud. They amassed vast wealth and influence in the New World that rivaled the grand palaces and empires they had built in the Old. The Silver Bloods had neither been seen nor heard from since Roanoke. As far as the ruling Conclave was concerned, Croatan were a myth; their existence legislated out of Blue Blood history.

In New York City, the Conclave leadership established the Committee, under whose aegis the vampires ran the Board of Trustees of the New York Blood Bank, among other educational institutions and charitable causes, as the Blue Bloods continued to advance their mission to bring art, light, truth, and justice to the human world.

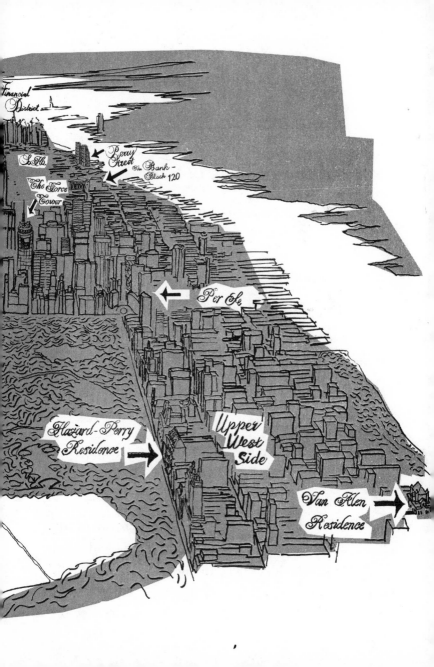

ONCE UPON A TIME IN NEW YORK . . .

our hundred years after the disappearance of the Roanoke colony, the mysterious attacks on the vampires began again. In New York City, Blue Blood victims were being taken during their most vulnerable period, their adolescence, before they are fully in control of their powers. Aggie Carondolet, a student at the Duchesne School, and four other teenagers, were fully consumed to Dissipation, their life force drained from their veins.

Half-blood vampire Schuyler Van Alen, along with her human Conduit, Oliver Hazard-Perry, and fellow Blue Blood Bliss Llewellyn, attempted to solve the murders and the disappearance of their friend Dylan Ward, who was charged with the crime. Schuyler's investigation brought her in contact with her secret crush, Jack Force, and to the malicious attention of his twin sister, Mimi. The Force twins hailed from the richest and most powerful Blue Blood family in the city. Their father, Charles Force, was the latest reincarnation of Michael, the vampires' immortal leader.

Schuyler learned the truth about the Silver Bloods from her grandmother Cordelia Van Alen, who was fatally injured after a Silver Blood ambush. Following Cordelia's last wish, Schuyler left for Venice to find her exiled grandfather. Lawrence Van Alen returned to New York to tell the Coven the same thing he had told them back in Plymouth as John Carver: he suspected that one of the oldest families of the Conclave had been Corrupted, and was hiding a powerful Silver Blood— perhaps the most powerful Silver Blood of all.

After Aggie's death, the Carondolets called for a White Vote to replace Charles Force, who was then the Regis of the Coven, their leader. They were unsuccessful in their attempt. Like the Carvers centuries before them, the Carondolets were promptly banished from the council. Charles Force refused to believe that the Silver Bloods had returned. He dismissed the deaths as random anomalies, not the work of their old, mythical foes.

But he could not stop the Committee from calling in the Venators, the Conclave's secret police force, to investigate the murders, sending one of them to enroll at Duchesne, the elite private school that many of the victims had attended. Kingsley Martin, the Venator assigned to the mission, was ordered to discover who among the young Blue Bloods had been drawn to the Dark Matter, a sign of Silver Blood Corruption. Mimi Force was the strongest suspect.

A Silver Blood attack at the Repository of History, the very center of the Blue Bloods power, left the Chief Warden murdered. Mimi was charged with the crime and brought to face a blood trial. Only a vampire with Gabrielle's power would be able to clear her by reading the true memories embedded in her blood. Schuyler, as Gabrielle's daughter, agreed to perform this act. In the blood memory, Schuyler discovered that Kingsley Martin, the Venator and allegedly a reformed Silver Blood, was the true culprit, and that Mimi was innocent. Schuyler also found out that Jack Force returned her feelings for him. But this discovery was complicated by the fact that she had recently performed the Sacred Kiss with Oliver Hazard-Perry, marking him as her human familiar, bound to her by blood and love.

Under Lawrence's influence, and after the embarrassment of the blood trial, the Conclave called for a White Vote, and for the first time since the Blue Bloods' banishment from the Kingdom of Heaven, Michael was no longer Regis, as Charles Force lost his position. They named Lawrence to lead them in his place.

Kingsley Martin disappeared after the trial, but was brought back to the fold when Lawrence discovered the truth behind his actions. Charles Force had secretly ordered the loyal Venator to call up a Silver Blood from deep inside their most protected stronghold. Kingsley, a reformed Silver Blood himself, had set up Mimi to perform the rite, but at the last moment she had been too weak, and he had performed the dark spell himself. According to Charles, the call should never have worked. It should have been impossible. It was a test that was supposed to have failed.

Now even Charles had to admit that their immortal adversaries had returned. A broken man, he turned his back on the Conclave, wasting his days locked up in his study. In his absence, Mimi promoted herself to the family seat in the council.

The Silver Blood attacks continued, and the

Venators reported trouble in Corcovado, where the demon Leviathan, Lucifer's brother, was imprisoned. Lawrence departed for Rio to secure Corcovado and left the Coven in the hands of the Regent, the second-highest-ranking Blue Blood, Nan Cutler.

Alone in New York, Schuyler had problems of her own. Her lost friend Dylan Ward had returned unexpectedly, displaying signs of Silver Blood Corruption, but her secret love affair with Jack Force took up all her attention and distracted her from the danger. But when the whole Conclave was called to Rio, Schuyler suspected something and traveled to the city as well, hoping to aid Lawrence.

During a dinner party to welcome the Blue Bloods to the city, the Silver Bloods revealed themselves at last and, led by the traitor Nan Cutler, slaughtered the members of the Conclave and left the house to burn with the Black Fire. Mimi barely made it out of the party alive, but it was her hand that felled the false Regent.

Schuyler and Lawrence rushed to Corcovado only to experience more grief. Through Lucifer's trickery, Leviathan was released and Lawrence slain. Before dying, Lawrence pressed Schuyler to fulfill his legacy and bring salvation back to their people. During the aftermath of Lawrence's murder, Bliss Llewellyn discovered a startling revelation about her provenance.

Back in New York, in the absence of a Regis, the Coven named Forsyth Llewellyn Regent, to preside over what was left of the Blue Blood leadership—a Conclave made up almost entirely of retired Elders and Wardens. They blamed Schuyler for causing Lawrence's death, and she fled New York with Oliver rather than face her sentence. Schuyler bade good-bye to Jack as well, for loving him could only lead to his doom.

Schuyler and Oliver traveled around the world, one step ahead of the Venators chasing them. In Paris, she was captured by no less than Jack Force himself. Meanwhile, Mimi had joined Kingsley's team to hunt for Jordan Llewellyn, who had been kidnapped by the Silver Bloods in Rio. Bliss, left at home in the Hamptons, desperately fought for the mastery of her soul.

Charles left for Paris to hunt Leviathan, only to get caught in his own trap. The Conclave, reduced to seven ruling houses, proposed a resolution reinstating Charles in the position of Regis when he returned. But Forsyth Llewellyn had other plans. He immediately called for a White Vote, nominating himself as Regis, under the orders of his true master, Lucifer.

Before the vote was tallied, Ambrose Barlow and Minerva Morgan, two of the oldest Wardens on the council, brought a damning anonymous letter about Forsyth to Mimi's attention. Mimi stalled on giving Forsyth leadership of the Conclave by withholding her approval.

Now, the Conclave remains leaderless in a time of great darkness. But there is a good omen at last: Allegra Van Alen finally awoke from her dreamless sleep with words of wisdom and hope for her two daughters, the light (Schuyler) and the shadow (Bliss).

As our story continues, the fate of the Blue Bloods rests in the hands of the newest generation of vampires and their loyal human Conduits. Can Schuyler, Jack, Oliver, Mimi, and Bliss work together to bring back peace and safety to their community? Or will Lucifer and his Silver Bloods destroy everything the Blue Bloods have worked so hard to build in their earthly home?

FAMILY RECORDS:
VAN ALEN

A formerly prominent New York family whose influence and largesse was instrumental in the founding of modern-day Manhattan, the Van Alen name was once synonymous with power, privilege, and patronage. But the family fortune has been dwindling for many years, now reduced to a few real estate holdings and nothing more.

SCHUYLER VAN ALEN

Half-blood

Birth Name: Schuyler Theodora Elizabeth Van Alen Chase

Origin: September 1, 1992, New York, New York

Known Past Lives: None: she is *Dimidium Cognatus* (half-human, half-vampire), the first and only one of her kind.

Bondmate: None. Schuyler is a trueborn new spirit with no heavenly past.

Assigned Human Conduit: Oliver Hazard-Perry

List of Human Familiars: Oliver Hazard-Perry, no others

Physical Characteristics:

    Hair: Black

    Eyes: Blue

    Height: 5'7"

Schuyler is the only daughter born to immortal mother, Allegra Van Alen (Gabrielle, the Uncorrupted) and mortal father, Stephen Chase, her mother's only human familiar. The Van Alens were once one of the community's wealthiest and most illustrious families, but fell on hard times when Allegra broke her blood bond to her brother Charles (Michael, Pure of Heart). Home is a shabby mansion on 101st Street and Riverside Drive. Other Van Alen holdings include a Nantucket compound, and a pied-à-terre in Paris (currently rented to visiting tourists).

Schuyler was born premature, and as a baby was perpetually underweight. Her pediatrician noted that she did not speak until her fourth birthday, when she suddenly began using whole sentences. Her primary caretaker, Cordelia Van Alen, her maternal grandmother, refused to allow speech therapy, insisting that her granddaughter was perfectly capable of speaking and would do so when she was ready.

School reports from Duchesne indicate that Schuyler was a quiet and thoughtful child, socially awkward, and if not for her best friend and human Conduit, Oliver Hazard-Perry, would have been a complete outcast. She excelled in Language Arts and Applied Arts, and was once honored by the faculty for diligence in her studies.

According to medical records from the Committee physician, Dr. Patricia Hazard, Schuyler's half-blood heritage means she has many powers that vampires her age do not, but also that her mixed blood makes her weaker and her Transformation to vampire unstable.

Her immortality is in question due to her human progenitor.

Schuyler's birth was a flagrant violation of the Code on her mother's part, and the Conclave has not yet come to a formal decision on her fate. Because it is said that the daughter of Gabrielle will bring the Blue Bloods the salvation they seek, Schuyler has been allowed to live. For now.

Schuyler Van Alen spends most of her time alone; she has a fondness for museums and long walks in Central Park, and made it a habit to revisit her comatose mother in the hospital every Sunday.

The following is a report from a Repository intern currently enrolled in Duchesne:

Intern Report #101

Schuyler Van Alen dresses like a nineteenth-century street urchin in thriftstore castoffs, but was recently tapped to be a model by New York's top agency during a casting call held at school. She gives the impression of being short of stature yet is in fact slightly taller than average. Her best friend, Oliver, calls her Sky, and according to a poem written in his diary (filched from his locker and scanned while subject was in class):

Her blue-black hair falls in curtains

Surrounding a delicate heart-shaped face

Blue eyes set deep in a pale, almost ivory

complexion

Stunning

Beautiful

Schuyler

Even those not so enamored will grudgingly accede that she is attractive. The beginnings of her Transformation came right on schedule in her fifteenth year, with the discovery of the sangre azul *on her forearms. Duly inducted into the Committee during the first semester of her sophomore year, she has displayed questionable judgment in the process of her Transformation. Her attendance at Committee meetings is inconsistent, and she recently performed the Sacred Kiss with her human Conduit, in a flagrant violation of Committee rules. According to Dr. Hazard, she had no other choice but to do so or she would have succumbed to a sickness and the loss of consciousness that felled her mother.*

Intern Report #202

While retiring in nature, Schuyler displays an unerring ability to attract the attention of the opposite sex. She was spotted dancing with Jack Force at the fall Informals, and rumors have it that her infatuation with Duchesne's most handsome and popular student may be returned. During the after-party at the Four Hundred Ball, she was spotted kissing a fellow masked reveler. Conflicting reports have the boy in question as Oliver Hazard-Perry, Kingsley Martin, or the most likely candidate, Jack Force.

Intern Report #303

Schuyler's infatuation/relationship with Jack Force appears to have grown since she was ordered to move to the Forces' town house after her adoption by her uncle, Charles Force. Several interns have confirmed sightings of Schuyler and Jack entering a residential building on Perry Street separately but within minutes of the other (real estate records show apartment 10 N. titled to the Benjamin Force Trust).

From a page from Schuyler's journal:

"To love Jack is to ruin him, to risk his very life. His eventual bonding with Mimi is law, it is life and death. I must leave him. I cannot keep doing this to Oliver, who loves me so much and whom I love as well. I cannot live with the guilt anymore. I have to say good-bye."

(Renfield's notes continued)

Schuyler Van Alen was put to a Committee hearing after the events in Rio, where Regis Lawrence Van Alen was murdered. She has been on the run for a year since the trial, but we can assume she returned to New York, as she was spotted at the bonding ceremony of Madeleine (Mimi) and Benjamin (Jack) Force at St. John's Cathedral.

We have pieced together the story and have discovered that Schuyler was hiding in the city under the name Skye Hope, using her shape-shifting abilities to pose as the daughter of an ex-hippie traveling singer.

Details on the events at St. John's are still coming to light. Eyewitness reports state that a silver mist appeared in the church, and the demon Leviathan himself abducted Schuyler, and they disappeared into the world of the glom. Venators on the scene reported that Jack and Mimi Force also disappeared at this time. Several minutes later, Jack and Schuyler emerged from the glom, Jack gravely injured and bleeding heavily. Guests at the scene testified they witnessed Schuyler offering her blood for him to drink. She was overheard telling him that as she was half human, that her blood could save him. Jack Force was then observed performing the Sacred Kiss on her, risking Corruption.

Schuyler was last seen at John F. Kennedy Airport with her faithful human Conduit/familiar, Oliver, but at the last moment, conflicting reports indicated that she entered the terminal with Jack Force, with Florence, Italy, as their possible intended destination.

Current Status: Missing. Suspected to have sought refuge in European Coven.

ALLEGRA VAN ALEN CHASE

Gabrielle, the Uncorrupted, the Virtuous,
the Messenger, Archangel of the Light
Birth Name: Allegra Elizabeth Van Alen
Origin: August 24, 1969, New York, New York
Known Past Lives: Rose Standish (Plymouth),
Tomasia Fosari (Florence), Junia Tertia (Rome), Meni
(Egypt)
Bondmate: Charles Force (broken). Bonded to
Stephen Chase (Red Blood)
Assigned Human Conduit: Warren Hazard-Perry
(deceased)
List of Human Familiars: Stephen Bendix Chase,
no others
Physical Characteristics:
    Hair: Blond
    Eyes: Green
    Height: 5'7"

Allegra Van Alen is the current reincarnation of Gabrielle, the Uncorrupted, one of only two of our kind who was not cursed or fallen, but became a vampire by choice instead of sin.

Like many Blue Bloods of her generation, she began

her education at the Duchesne School in Manhattan but transferred to Endicott Academy, a boarding school in Massachusetts, during her junior year. As a student, Allegra was known on campus as cheerful, spirited, and athletic; captain of the girls' field hockey team and a natural-born leader. She made a stunning debut at the Four Hundred Ball on her eighteenth year, leading the cotillion with her brother, Charles. *Town & Country* christened her the "debutante of the decade."

As far as the Repository is concerned, nothing in Allegra's past or her personality suggested that she was capable of violating the Code in a most egregious manner. When she came of age at twenty-one (not eighteen, as previously believed: see new documents updating Allegra's history/diary/Hazard-Perry notes), Allegra forsook her blood bond to her bondmate and vampire twin, Charles Force (Michael, Pure of Heart: see Force Family Files/Angelus Files/Pure) to elope with her human familiar, Stephen Chase. The marriage remains the only instance of a vampire-human bonding. The couple lived in hiding for several years until Charles Force, acting from his position as Regis of the Conclave, lifted the sanction and allowed Allegra to return to the Coven.

Allegra succumbed to a self-imposed coma in 1995, three years following the birth of her half-human daughter, who was conceived from the illegal union with her husband/human familiar. While earlier reports indicated that Allegra lapsed into unconsciousness immediately following the birth of her child, the Repository has concluded that the confusion on the dates of Allegra's current long-term hospitalization stemmed from her lengthy stay at the maternity ward after the difficult birth of her child. The date of that earlier internment (9/1/1992) was mistakenly applied as the date of her remittance into the care facility.

It is speculated that sorrow from the death of her human husband {DEATH UNCONFIRMED-RENFIELD} was what led Allegra to lapse into a comatose state. She would not participate in the *Caerimonia Osculor* with any other human after their bonding, and when he died, she chose to withdraw from life as well.

A recent visit to her hospital bed revealed that even at forty years of age, Allegra has kept her incandescent beauty. While most of the community used to visit at her bedside, in recent years, only two visitors have signed the security logs: her estranged bondmate, Charles Force, and her daughter, Schuyler Van Alen.

While some in the Coven believe that Charles Force could use his considerable influence on his twin to wake her, he himself has admitted that he has no such power over her reduced state.

From Hospital Records

DATE REDACTED BY ORDER OF REGIS
—An orderly working the late shift reported that he heard screaming from patient's room.

—Patient undisturbed. (Orderly delusional?)

—Security logs indicate visit from her daughter. But signature is of a B. Llewellyn? (Is this correct? Reconfirm with security.)

DATE REDACTED BY ORDER OF REGIS
—Patient awake and coherent.
Alert: Dr. Patricia Hazard

—Daughter visit. (S. Van Alen)

DATE REDACTED BY ORDER OF REGIS
—Patient missing.

CONFIDENTIAL,
From Lawrence Van Alen Records

This letter was found among Allegra Van Alen's personal effects.

My daughter,

If you are reading this, you are awake. I am writing, for I fear we shall not meet in this lifetime or in any other. I am leaving for Rio tomorrow evening, and I do not know if I will be able to return.

Before I left, I wanted to finally answer the question you posed to me before I went into exile. Yes, you did have a child in {REDACTED}. We kept her hidden from you after her birth, and her destruction was my doing. I cannot speak for Charles, but I ask you to forgive him for the sin we committed so many centuries ago. He did only *what I asked of him, for the good of the Coven.*

I leave you as ever, your loving father,
Lawrence

TOP SECRET
Conclave-level Only

Gabrielle birthed many reincarnated spirits in many cycles. She is, in a sense, mother to all, but we have recently learned that she had not one but two trueborn daughters: children who were created as new spirits and not simply a reincarnation of an immortal one. (So far, Gabrielle is the only vampire able to procreate in the human sense. No other vampire female has been able to create new life instead of carrying the immortal spirits of those who came before.)

The House of Records has always been aware of Schuyler Van Alen, but only recently has been apprised of the continued existence of Allegra's other daughter, one born during {REDACTED}. The child was to have been destroyed by order of the Regis. New information indicates that Cordelia Van Alen may have been correct in her assumption that the child survived as a result of treachery within the Conclave. With the disappearance of Forsyth Llewellyn during the attack at St. John the Divine, and recent documents previously suppressed by Warden Cutler that show Bliss Llwellyn carried the mark of Lucifer on her neck, the Conclave has come to the conclusion that Bliss Llewellyn is Allegra's firstborn daughter (the product of Allegra's union with Lucifer) and a Silver Blood. The Repository is still in the dark as to how this came to be.

Current Status: Missing. Suspected to be searching for Charles Force in the White Darkness.

(For more on Allegra's story see *Misguided Angel*, Repository Record #505, which contains the comprehensive file on the many lives of Gabrielle.)

CORDELIA VAN ALEN

Seraphiel, Angel of Song

Birth Name: Cordelia Edith Benjamin

Origin: August 12, 1841, New York, New York

Known Past Lives: Catherine Carver (Plymouth), Isabella Arosto (Florence), Julia Caesaris (Rome)

Bondmate: Lawrence Van Alen

Assigned Human Conduit: James Owen Perry (deceased)

List of Human Familiars: Anthony Smith (1919–1925), David Lancaster (1926–1943), Tobias West (1943–1969), Dmitri Stefan (1969–1982), Kenneth Lindsey (1983–1999), Rigoberto Morales [also her hairdresser] (1999–2006)

Physical Characteristics:

    Hair: White (blond in her younger years)

    Eyes: Green

    Height: 5′2″

Cordelia Van Alen was, until her untimely expiration, the matriarch of the Van Alen family. She was Schuyler's grandmother and acted as her legal guardian after Allegra fell into a coma. One of the Coven's longest-serving Wardens, Cordelia nevertheless found herself in a diminished position in the Conclave after she clashed once too often with the ruling Elders.

Born in 1841, Cordelia was a precocious child, and in her youth was known for her lovely soprano singing voice. She married Lawrence Van Alen in 1859 in a lavish bonding ceremony at the Van Alen mansion on Fifth Avenue. She was allowed to go beyond three times the normal human life span to prepare as the next mother to the Uncorrupted, Allegra and Charles, whose spirits were entrusted to her guidance according to the laws of the House of Records in 1969.

Throughout Blue Blood history, Cordelia, along with her exiled bondmate, Lawrence, has been agitating for increased vigilance against the possible return of the {REDACTED} {REINSTATED/BY ORDER OF THE REGIS LVA} Silver Bloods. {ALL REDACTED MENTION OF SILVER BLOODS REINSTATED IN CURRENT RECORDS BY ORDER OF THE REGIS LVA} She was instrumental in calling up the spirit of the Watcher, the Pistis Sophia, in this cycle, to be born to and fostered by the family of Forsyth Llewellyn.

During her long tenure as one of New York City's most active social matrons, Cordelia presided over the New York Blood Bank Committee, the Central Park

Conservancy, and served on the board of trustees for the Metropolitan Museum of Art, the Museum of Modern Art, New York City Ballet, and the New York Philharmonic.

Elegant, birdlike, and imperious, Cordelia was intimidating and aloof in manner, even in her relations with her granddaughter. However, she always avowed to intimates among the Coven that while she was instrumental in many great causes and charities, her greatest joy in life was watching Schuyler grow up.

Cordelia was attacked by a powerful young Silver Blood during the New York slayings of 2006, but fortunately did not suffer from Full Consumption. Before her "death," she pressed upon Schuyler to find her grandfather, Lawrence Van Alen, whom Cordelia guessed was still living in Venice.

Current Status: Expired in this cycle. Will return in the next Expression.

LAWRENCE VAN ALEN

Metraton, Heavenly Scribe

Birth Name: Lawrence Theodore Winslow Van Alen
(also called "Teddy")

Origin: Enmortal. Does not adhere to the cycle of
Expression and Expiration.

Known Past Lives: John Carver (Plymouth),
Ludivivo Arosto (Florence), Gnaeus Magnus Pompey
(Rome)

Bondmate: Cordelia Van Alen

Assigned Human Conduit: Christopher Anderson

List of Human Familiars: Unknown

Physical Characteristics:

    Hair: White (blond in his younger years)

    Eyes: Blue

    Height: 6'0"

Until recent events cleared his name and reputation,
Lawrence Van Alen was considered by many in the
Coven to be an agitator, a traitor, and a troublemaker.
Upon the founding of the New World, as John Carver,
he lost his prominent position in the Conclave after los-
ing the White Vote. The council had voted to follow
Myles Standish (Michael), as they have always done,

regardless of the suspected return of the Silver Bloods.

Lawrence was a prodigious reader and writer of historical books, and was the founding director of the Repository of History. Many of the books in our library are from his personal collection. During his tenure as Committee Warden (1710–1790), he made the secondary and collegiate education of young Blue Bloods a necessary provision to their progression, regardless of their ability to remember the knowledge gleaned from past cycles. According to his speech before the Conclave, "Blue Bloods must understand our place in the world before we can attempt to change it. You may be able to call up an entire encyclopedia, but nothing is more meaningless than a brain with no heart and no reasoning."

An Enmortal, he bonded to Cordelia Benjamin in 1859 and disappeared from the Coven's records after his self-imposed exile around 1873 (dates still unconfirmed). According to Cordelia's diaries, they had decided to separate, believing that Lawrence would be safer conducting his research on his own. For as long as he lived, he believed that the Silver Bloods had infiltrated the highest echelons of the Conclave.

According to Conduit Hazard-Perry's notes, Lawrence was hiding in plain sight as a professor of linguistics and history at the University of Venice. Upon his return to the New York Coven after the attack at the Repository, Lawrence immediately called for the White Vote and won the title of Regis. During his brief tenure as head of the Coven, he opened up the Repository Files on the Croatan/Silver Bloods and was instrumental in allowing the Venator teams to re-form and return to their full power in order to meet the growing threat of the Silver Bloods' return.

During his investigation into troubling events in Rio de Janeiro, Lawrence was slain, allegedly by Leviathan himself. Eyewitnesses at the scene are not credible: Bliss Llewellyn does not remember anything, Oliver Hazard-Perry is human (Red Blood testimony is inadmissible), and Schuyler Van Alen is a person of interest in the investigation and has yet to be brought in front of a full tribunal to ascertain the truths of the events on the night in question.

Lawrence's prodigious research notes, labeled only *Van Alen, Legacy—Paths,* have been missing since his Conduit retired from service. It is the Repository's belief

that these documents are now in the hands of Schuyler
Van Alen.

Current Status. Finished. (If the
Conclave is to believe Schuyler's
account, the Enmortal has been
extinguished forever from the Light.)

STEPHEN CHASE

Human Familiar
Birth Name: Stephen Bendix Chase
Origin: September 1, 1967, San Francisco, California
Bondmate: Allegra Van Alen Chase
Physical Characteristics: (according to high school records)
  Hair: Blond
  Eyes: Blue
  Height: 6'3"

Not much is known about Stephen Chase, Schuyler Van Alen's Red Blood father. In fact, according to the official records, his name is misspelled with a "V" ("Steven Chase" according to the Van Alen family tree in *Masquerade* [Repository Record #202]). This could be a result of Allegra Van Alen's hope to keep the identity of her human familiar a secret, or a result of a common clerical error. Allegra always maintained that she met Stephen, an artist in San Francisco, at his gallery opening in 1990. However, new documents unearthed by a research team led by Oliver Hazard-Perry (which include Allegra's high school diary) indicate that they may have met earlier. It has just come to light that Stephen Chase may have been the same person as Bendix Chase, a boy who was in the same year as Allegra at Endicott Academy, a boarding school in Massachusetts. If so, then Ben/Stephen was her first and only human familiar.

In any event, in the fall of 1990, Allegra made Stephen her bondmate, against the Code of the Vampires, breaking her blood bond to her brother, Charles. His name appears on Schuyer Van Alen's birth certificate, but it is unknown whether he lived to see his daughter. The documents are unclear on the time of his death, again, perhaps a deliberate deception on Allegra Van Alen's part—it is our belief that she did not want the Committee to know very much about her human husband, and many documents pertaining to his whereabouts are missing or were destroyed. We can only assume that he is dead, as he has never been in contact with either his comatose wife or his errant daughter.

Current Status: Presumed deceased

OLIVER HAZARD-PERRY

Human Familiar/Human Conduit
Birth Name: Oliver Aloysius Fitzgerald
Hazard-Perry II
Origin: October 18, 1992, New York, New York
Physical Characteristics:
    Hair: Brown
    Eyes: Hazel
    Height: 5′11″

Born to one of the oldest human families in service to the vampires, Oliver Hazard-Perry was assigned to Schuyler Van Alen from the moment of his birth. Like all human Conduits, Oliver has been trained in the art of secrecy and vassalage. He has performed admirably well, and as Schuyler's human Conduit, Oliver has gone above and beyond the call of duty. It is noted that he is not only her best friend, but her confidant, protector, and "partner in crime," according to a Repository intern posted at Duchesne. However, he displayed uncharacteristically poor judgment by allowing her to take him as her human familiar, marking him with the Sacred Kiss, an offense that has so far gone unpunished, due to an order from the Regis (Lawrence Van Alen, 2007).

Oliver is an exceptional student at Duchsene, with one of the highest human IQ's recorded for his generation. His academic performance has been stellar, although his participation in athletics has been the minimum required of a Conduit. He is a frequent visitor to museums and galleries, and is one of the youngest important collectors of antiquities in the world.

The Repository has long suspected that Oliver was instrumental in aiding and abetting Schuyler Van Alen's yearlong evasion from Committee justice. However, the Committee is satisfied with his confession, and further investigation into the possibly illegal nature of his actions has been terminated. (Note: The Hazard-Perry family recently made a sizable donation into the Committee's accounts.)

He was rumored to have been spotted at Kennedy Airport with Schuyler Van Alen the day after the Silver Blood attack at St. John's Cathedral. However, details remain inconclusive, as conflicting eyewitnesses report that she was last seen with Jack Force, entering the International Terminal. Under the Vampire–Conduit Confidentiality Act of 1755, Oliver will not confirm or deny any of our suspicions of Schuyler Van Alen's actions or whereabouts. In any event, with Schuyler missing, Oliver has been relieved of his duties as human Conduit and has chosen to serve the Committee in another position.

Current Status: Repository Scribe

Author's Note: A request—more like a plea—I receive very often from my readers is to tell the story of Schuyler and Jack's first meeting at the Perry Street apartment. So I thought I would write it, since I wanted to see it for myself.

THERE'S A FIRST (OR FOURTH) TIME FOR EVERYTHING, OR "MR. DARCY REQUESTS"
Schuyler's Story

When Schuyler awoke that morning, she found that a book had been slipped underneath her door. It was wedged tightly in the narrow space, and she had to pull it out carefully so it wouldn't bend or catch. *The Plague* by Albert Camus. She held it up and flipped through the yellowed pages. Inside the book was an envelope, and inside the envelope was a key. There was nothing else—no note, no address, nothing. Schuyler had no idea what the key was for, but she had an inkling that she should not ask Mimi about it.

She retrieved an old pair of Doc Martens from her

trunk and removed one of the frayed shoelaces. She looped one end of the shoelace through the key and tied it around her neck so that it hung underneath her shirt collar, hidden. The book she put away in her backpack. She had read *The Plague* for class the year before and had not liked it very much; had found it depressing and severe. Why had *he* chosen to give her a copy? Because, of course, the moment she picked it up, she knew who had given her the book—there was no one else in the Force town house that even cared that she lived there now.

She tried to remember the story of *The Plague*: a terrible epidemic strikes a small town, which is then quarantined from the rest of the world. One of the main characters is separated from his wife—whom he longs for throughout the novel. He struggles to hold on, fighting despair only because he so desperately wants to see her again. Schuyler's heart began to beat a little too fast. Was it possible that she was reading too much into this? Certainly. She tried to remember what she had learned in Mr. Orion's English class. Wasn't Camus's story one of social breakdown and the futility of the human condition? *The Plague* was a story about rats and disease, wasn't it? But what had *he* argued . . . Oh, she remembered now . . . He had argued that the story was about longing and exile . . . and love.

So what? Schuyler thought, running a hairbrush through her dark hair before pulling it back into a ponytail. So what if he'd given her a book and key? She was still miserable. She was still living with *them* and not her grandfather. Ever since she'd arrived, she had been made to feel as welcome as Jane Eyre at Gateshead with her rich cousins. She was lucky that Mimi hadn't locked her in the closet yet.

And so what if he'd kissed her the day before? His kisses meant nothing. He had kissed her and run off three times now—the first at a party, the second at the masquerade ball, and the third in her bedroom yesterday. It was just yesterday. She tried to shake off the memory, pulled on her coat and headed downstairs. She wanted to leave while the house was still quiet; she didn't want to risk bumping into anyone, wanted the chance to slip away as quietly as possible without anyone noticing.

She walked out and took a deep breath of fresh air. She couldn't understand him. What did he want? He was bonded to Mimi, wasn't he? And yet he had kissed her yesterday afternoon, and then had disappeared so quickly she had to assume he was repulsed by her, or perhaps repulsed by his attraction to her, which was just as humiliating. Maybe he only liked her when no one else was looking. . . . Maybe he was just playing a game . . . toying with her emotions while she churned with confusion and desire. . . .

Three stolen kisses—it didn't add up to anything, really. He was never going to be her boyfriend, she thought as she turned right onto 96th Street. He was never going to sling his arm around her as they walked down the hall, never take her to Winter Ball, never declare his love over the PA system by mangling the lyrics to "Come on Eileen," as Jamie Kip had done so charmingly last week when he'd serenaded Ally Elly, before the head girl had cut him off. But Schuyler didn't want any of that—did she? She had never yearned for popularity. It struck her as absurd anyway, to want popularity. Popularity was fickle and elusive, like trying to catch fireflies in a jar. You were either born with it or relegated to wallflower status according to the mysterious and unknowable workings of the universe.

It wasn't something you strove for or wished for or worked for, no matter how many silly articles and teenage novels and Hollywood movies tried to convince you otherwise. Popularity was something other people decided *for* you—other people decided you were fun and pretty and interesting and wanted to be your friend. Hence, you were popular. Most people thought Schuyler was weird, and left her alone.

She arrived at school early and ate her breakfast by her locker. She'd brought a yogurt and banana taken from the Forces' immaculate commercial refrigeration system (nothing so bourgeois as a fridge, of course; this was the size of a small closet). Classes wouldn't start for another half hour yet, and she relished having the place to herself. Soon enough, the hallways would be filled with the sound of gossip and camaraderie, and Schuyler would feel even lonelier than when she was alone. It was so much easier when no one was around.

As much as she was not the kind of girl who wished he would claim her as his own in front of everyone to see, a little part of her could not help but wish for it nonetheless. The problem with being alienated is that one is never alienated enough, she thought as students began to trickle in before the first bell. She could swath herself in black clothes and hide behind her hair, shut off the rest of the world and listen to angry music on her iPod, but somehow it was all a pose, wasn't it? Was she just a poser? Because why was she drawn to him, then, the kind of boy that every girl wanted to date? Didn't that mean she was just like everyone else? If only she didn't care so much; but she did. At heart, behind the quiet and the scowl and the indifference, she cared very, very much.

And then, there he was. Right in the middle of a group of laughing, joking boys—always right in the center, the tallest and handsomest one—the one you couldn't help but stare at. . . .

Jack Force. He must have just gotten back from crew practice on the Hudson. She could always tell when he had been rowing; she could smell the sea air on his skin, in his hair, his cheeks were ruddy and flushed. He looked happy. For the briefest second he caught her eye—but then turned away.

Schuyler bent down to her books, biting her bottom lip. She had just imagined it, hadn't she? The kisses, everything. They didn't exist in the real world. In the real world, she and Jack were strangers. She wasn't looking, and someone jostled her elbow so that she lost her grip on her bookbag, and the book—*The Plague*—tumbled out, and she thought, If this is what some people think is a love story, they are just kidding themselves.

But aren't all stories about love in some way?

Schuyler startled to hear Jack's voice in her head, and looked up, but the hallway was empty. The second bell rang, and she was late.

Only the good ones, only the good stories, she thought, wondering if he could hear her, if he was listening.

The next morning, another book had been slipped underneath her door. What was this all about? Was he building her a library? This time, since the book was too thick to fit completely, it had been shoved, stuffed in the opening between the door and the floor, halfway in and halfway out, so that when Schuyler pulled it out, the paperback was bent in the middle and the pages were creased. *Pride and Prejudice* by Jane Austen. This time, inside the book there was a note.

173 Perry Street. #10 N. Midnight. Use the key.

She touched the key that hung around her neck, for luck. *The Plague* yesterday. Now *Pride and Prejudice*. Was it an alphabetical choice? she wondered, amused. Talk about a love story. *Pride and Prejudice*—so obvious, wasn't it? Schuyler had always been skeptical of its pull until she had spent a long, heady weekend wrapped up in the joys of its combative romance. Elizabeth and Darcy don't so much fall in love as fight their attraction every step of the way. Schuyler had come to love the book despite her misgivings, to hold its promise of carriages and Pemberley to her chest as stoutly as she believed that Elizabeth should have inherited the carriages and the estate on her own. It was so difficult to imagine such a stringent, corseted world for women; to imagine a life completely dependent on one's ability to land the right guy. Still, there was something deeply appealing about such a story. It made the romance so much more . . . What did they call it? High stakes.

In any event, *Pride and Prejudice* was way more appealing than *The Plague*.

Feeling reckless and giddy, and just a tad *plucky*—like the kind of girl who tramped around the marshes in the dark—she scribbled a note and slipped it under Jack's door.

Mr. Darcy, I will be there as requested. —Elizabeth

At midnight, Schuyler slipped the key in the lock and turned it. The apartment was dark, which made the view from the floor-to-ceiling windows even more breathtaking, the dark river against city lights, the West Side Highway a ribbon of yellow taxicabs. Schuyler stepped inside and looked around. She closed the door behind her. But she was alone. No one was there.

And then, before she could breathe, there he was, solid, against her, his warm lips on hers, his hands around her waist, and she had dropped the key and the book on the floor. She wanted to cry out—to ask questions—but she could feel his heart beating against hers and the intensity of the emotion exploding between them. She returned his kisses with an ardor that she did not know she was capable of—and he buried his face in her neck as if he wanted to breathe in every part of her—and she buckled to the floor so that he fell with her, until they were lying down, still kissing, their bodies entwined like roots of a tree.

"Jack . . ." she finally said, when she had found her voice. He was lying on top of her, his weight heavy and yet light at the same time—a weight she wanted to bear. "I . . ." She wanted to tell him the same thing she had wanted to tell him since that night when he first kissed her. He had stopped her from saying it back then, but he wouldn't stop her now. She wanted him to know how she felt about him.

Jack looked at her and raised an eyebrow. He looked so serious in the moonlight, but his eyes were teasing.

They were sparkling. This was a boy who spoke through books: longing and exile—*The Plague*—banter and obstacles—*Pride and Prejudice*. He spoke her language. She watched as he, with his hair tousled and his eyes shining, raised her arms above her head so that she was immobile beneath him. The strength in his hold and the exquisite torture of wondering when he would kiss her again was too much to bear. It was painful to feel so much desire.

Then he bent down and kissed her gently, a feathery whisper that melted against her as she pressed her body against his.

She knew right then that she didn't have to say anything.

They understood each other perfectly.

There would never be anything but this. Stolen moments, stolen kisses, a secret oasis. There would be no public displays of affection. In school and at his home, there would only be indifference and detachment. There would be no holding hands, no study dates, no dinner dates, no dates at all. Ever.

But it was all right. She would take as much as he could give, and for now, it was enough.

HÔTEL LAMBERT – THE ARRIVAL OF THE ELEPHANTS

FAMILY RECORDS:
FORCE

Charles Van Alen changed his family name to "Force" after his bondmate and twin sister, Allegra Van Alen, broke their blood bond to bond with her human familiar. From his actions we can only conclude that he no longer considered himself a member of the Van Alen family, and thus we have created a new family record to reflect his new allegiance.

JACK FORCE

Abbadon, Angel of Destruction, Twin Angel of the Apocalypse, the Unlikely, Destroyer of Worlds

Birth Name: Benjamin Hamilton Force, known as "Jack"

Origin: June 7, 1991, New York, New York

Known Past Lives: Henry Searle (Newport), William White (Plymouth), Louis d'Orleans (Versailles), Valerius (Rome)

Bondmate: Madeleine Force (presumed broken)

Assigned Human Conduit: None

List of Human Familiars: Kitty Mullins (2006)

Physical Characteristics:

    Hair: Blond (platinum)

    Eyes: Green

    Height: 6'2"

As a child, Benjamin Force was known for his uncontrollable temper tantrums and was given the nickname "Blackjack," which was then shortened to "Jack." In elementary school, Jack was a whirlwind of activity, unable to sit still or concentrate, and was diagnosed by human psychiatrists as having Attention Deficit Disorder and was prescribed copious amounts of antianxiety medication. His symptoms disappeared once the Transformation took hold, however, and since then he has been a model student.

Intern Report #102

Jack Force is captain of the lacrosse team; lead in every school play (Konstantin in The Seagull *and Melchior in* Spring Awakening*); described as "painfully handsome" by most of the female population (the usual: tall, platinum-haired, chiseled good looks, piercing green eyes, athletic, graceful, etc . . .). Jack performs at a stellar academic and athletic level. He is a natural leader to his peers, and only in comparison to his more loquacious twin does he come across as reticent and taciturn. Those who know him well describe him as funny and charming, and never to be found without a book in his hand. Jack is a frequent visitor to the Repository library.*

(Renfield's notes continued)

At the Four Hundred Ball, Jack was revealed as Abbadon, the Angel of Destruction, a position traditionally known as God's Enforcer, the hammer blow, his duty and burden to remind man of his mortality. In the current cycle, his bondmate, Azrael, was revealed to be his twin sister, Mimi. Known together as the Angels of the Apocalypse, the Force twins are of one mind, two sides of one coin, blood bound in Heaven, and destined to find each other and renew their vows in every cycle. Reports of Abbadon's infatuation with Gabrielle are unfounded but persistent. In any event, for centuries innumerable, he has remained true to Azrael. Jack took a sabbatical from Duchesne for a year, and reports recently made available to the Repository indicate that he was on a secret Venator mission with Charles Force to hunt Leviathan in Paris.

Jack has been missing since the day of his scheduled bonding to Mimi at the Cathedral of St. John the Divine. While he was feared lost during the Silver Blood attack, conflicting eyewitness reports state that he was spotted emerging from the glom, critically injured but intact. He then allegedly performed the Sacred Kiss on none other than Schuyler Van Alen, whose mixed blood, we can safely assume, saved his life. The next day he was observed again in her company at the international terminal at Kennedy Airport. If we are to believe the intern reports, Jack had been conducting a secret affair with Schuyler for several months.

Breaking his bond with his vampire twin is in direct violation of the Code of the Vampires, and if spotted within the territory of the New York Coven, he must immediately be brought to justice, and faces a sentence of death from his twin.

Current Status: Missing. Believed to be in the company of Schuyler Van Alen and to have sought refuge in the European Coven.

MIMI FORCE

Azrael, Angel of Death, Twin Angel of the
Apocalypse

Birth Name: Madeleine Alexis Force, known as
"Mimi"

Origin: June 7, 1991, New York, New York

Known Past Lives: Eliza Whitney (Newport),
Susannah Fuller (Plymouth), Elisabeth Lorraine-
Lillebonne (Versailles), Agrippina (Rome)

Bondmate: Jack Force (presumed broken)

Assigned Human Conduit: None

List of Human Familiars: See pages 84–88 in
Records of Human Interaction for full list. (Too many
to mention here; number in possible violation of
the Code.)

Phyiscal Characteristics:

    Hair: Blond (platinum)

    Eyes: Green

    Height: 5'9"

Dubbed "the most beautiful girl in the history of New
York City," Mimi Force is a social luminary, a tabloid
favorite, and a local celebrity. A file on Mimi Force
would be remiss if it did not include a description of
her comely physical attributes: long platinum hair, skin

the color of fresh milk, sloelike emerald green eyes, and that famous twenty-two-inch waist.

At Duchesne, Mimi is an indifferent student, but has consistently shown promise as one of the most talented in the new generation of vampires. However, she can be arrogant and regularly bends the rules concerning human familiars, putting them at risk for Full Consumption. The queen of her social circle at Duchesne, Mimi reportedly took Bliss Llewellyn into her acquaintance at the orders of her father. Mimi concerns herself with superficial pursuits and can often be found at pricey clothing stores or in the banquettes of the latest nightclub.

Blood bound to her cycle brother, Jack, Mimi has been observed to exhibit frustration, desperation, and rage at her twin's increasing (alleged) obsession with Schuyler Van Alen. Mimi was the prime suspect of the Venator investigation in the attack at the Repository and the murder of Warden Priscilla Dupont. She was cleared at a blood trial when Venator Martin was shown to have called the Silver Blood.

Mimi's frivolous façade obscures the fact that Azreal is one of history's most fearsome hunters of Silver Blood spawn. As the Committee's newest minted Venator, she is a talented Truth Seeker and joined the team that found the remains of Jordan Llewellyn in Brazil. During this tenure she was rumored to have conducted an intimate affair with her commanding officer, Venator Martin. However, the veracity of this gossip is doubtful, as upon her return to New York, Mimi took no time in enthusiastically planning her bonding to Jack. When her father resigned from the Conclave, Mimi claimed the family seat and serves as her family's voice on the council.

Mimi survived the attack at the cathedral, but her brother's sudden disappearance and rumored liaison with Schuyler Van Alen has compelled her to call for his execution, as proscribed by the Code of the Vampires. The punishment for breaking a heavenly promise is eternal death. The *Castigatio Mortis* can only be called for by the bondmate. While Charles Force did not call for this punishment on Allegra Van Alen, Mimi has no qualms in her decision. She has been overheard saying, "If I ever see Jack again, I'm going to kill him."

Current Status: Conclave elder. Venator emerita.

CHARLES FORCE

Michael, Pure of Heart, the Valiant, Prince of the Angels, Supreme Commander of the Lord's Armies, Archangel of the Light

Birth Name: Charles Edgar Van Alen

Origin: August 24, 1969, New York, New York (*Blue Bloods*: Repository Record #101 lists his age as sixty. This is incorrect and possibly the result of Charles's hair going prematurely silver.)

Known Past Lives: Myles Standish (Plymouth), Cassius (Rome), Menes (Egypt)

Bondmate: Allegra Van Alen (broken)

Cycle Wife: Trinity Burden

Assigned Human Conduit: Virgil Hazard-Perry (recused from service by CF, 1990)

List of Human Familiars: Georgina Guest (1987–1988), Susan King (1989–1991), Charlotte Pittman (1992–1995), Desiree Hutch (1991–1994), Sidney Cohen (1995–1999), Aspeth Heimann (2000–2003), Gina Dupont (2003–2006), current human familiar unknown

Physical Characteristics:

    Hair: Silver (formerly black)

    Eyes: Gray

    Height: 5′10″

Charles Force is the latest reincarnation of Michael, the Blue Bloods' leader since time immemorial. In this cycle he divested his share of the Van Alen trust to build a new multimedia company. His Force News Network spans the globe and wields an incomparable influence upon every aspect of human interaction, from news to politics to sports to entertainment. He serves on the board of several Fortune 500 companies and was instrumental in the election of Forsyth Llewellyn to the U.S. Senate. As Regis, he expanded the funding for the New York Blood Bank for medical research on blood-borne diseases; founded the New York Institute for Policy Research, a conservative think tank; and is known as a major donor to the Republican Party.

Educated at Endicott Academy, Harvard College, and Harvard Business School, Charles Force's life has been marred by the inexplicable breaking of the bond between himself and his twin sister, Allegra Van Alen. All reports of their early life together indicated that they were ready and willing to commit to their union, as they have for centuries past, until the jarring and unfortunate decision on Allegra's part to elope with her human familiar, Stephen Chase.

After Allegra broke their bond, Charles engaged in

a human marriage with Trinity Burden (Sandalphon), who lost her bondmate in the Great War. In 1990, he petitioned the House of Records to allow him to call up the spirits of Azrael and Abbadon as his twin children, Mimi and Jack Force.

Charles Force recently won a custody battle in the Red Blood courts that allowed him to overturn Cordelia Van Alen's petition to make Schuyler Van Alen an emancipated minor. For a time, Schuyler Van Alen was fostered in his home.

After he was deposed as Regis, Charles withdrew from Blue Blood life, and was reported to spend his days locked in his study. After Lawrence's alleged death, Charles disappeared but was sighted at the *Bal des Vampires* at the Hôtel Lambert. If Venator reports are to be believed, he was last seen locked in a furious battle with the demon Leviathan and was lost when the Silver Blood released the *subvertio*.

```
Current Status: Missing. Believed to be
lost in the White Darkness.
```

TRINITY BURDEN FORCE

Sandalphon, The Angel of Silence
Birth Name: Trinity Amelia Burden
Origin: February 11, 1971, New York, New York
Known Past Lives: Janice Adelaide (Melbourne),
Sorina Sedlak (Prague), Claudia Caepionis (Rome)
Bondmate: Salgiel (deceased)
Assigned Human Conduit: None
List of Human Familiars: Greer Chapman
(1989–1990), Oswald Hefferlin (1990–1995), Paul
Thornton (1995–1997), Simon Lawlor (1999–2005),
Boone Mitchell (2005–present)

Cycle wife to Charles Force and cycle mother to the twins, Trinity Force was instrumental in the founding of the Committee and is well known in New York society for her exquisite taste and good breeding. She lost her bondmate, Salgiel, during the Great War in Rome and was free to marry Charles, in the Red Blood sense, after Allegra broke her heavenly bond. Theirs is a marriage of convenience rather than true affection, and it was rumored that Charles chose her as his bride for the considerable dowry she brought to the marriage.

Until Charles's disappearance led her to take leadership of the Force News Network, Trinity was like many a Park Avenue matron—a benefactress of the arts, opera, and discreet plastic surgery.

> Current Status: Committee warden

Author's Note: This is a companion story to Revelations. *It details Schuyler and Jack's final encounter, from Jack's perspective. Schuyler has come back from Rio and has agreed to meet Jack at the Perry Street apartment. The Committee is in disarray. Lawrence and many of the top-ranking members of the Coven have been murdered. This event happened before the epilogue, in which Jack and Mimi reunite.*

THE LIE THAT CONCEALED THE TRUTH, OR "THE LAST MEETING"

Jack's Story

It is my turn to wait. Funny that in all these months we have been meeting, it was always she who waited for me. It was never my intention to make her wait, but my path to this place has always been the more complicated one.

I flip through the pages of *Anna Karenina*. The book I had slipped under her door before she left the country.

The book that I found in my locker this morning, returned to me. A sign that *she* wanted to meet. She has never done this before. The light is good here—I can see all of downtown from the windows. The city is still and quiet outside. There are no cabs honking, no dogs barking, no ambulances wailing; instead, all is silent. An eerie calm.

The door opens slowly. The moment I see her face I know something is wrong. I expected it, and yet I am still wounded by it. She does not fly into my arms as before, and her eyes are clouded and gray. She displays none of that happiness to see me that I took so much delight in for so long. Only a grim acceptance.

"I am sorry about your grandfather," I say. "Your loss is shared by all." Words are not enough; they can only do what words can do. Lawrence was more than a friend; he was a mentor, an ally. I grieve his loss deeply.

When the news came—that Corcovado had broken, that Leviathan walks the earth once again—I did not react as many of us did, with shock and fear. Instead I felt the old blood in these veins stir with vengeance. We will avenge each of our lost brothers and sisters. *Worldbreaker* is waiting. We will not despair or retreat. We will fight. And we will win. War has come to us once again, and this time we will vanquish our foes for eternity. I am almost looking forward to it.

"Do not worry, my love, we shall have our vengeance. I promise it. Lawrence will not have died in vain."

Her eyes become bright. She nods curtly. "He died because of me."

"He died to protect you. It was his duty."

She stands so still at the doorway, as if she doesn't know what to do or what to say. And yet I know already. She will tell me we must stop meeting because the Coven will need me now, and that she will be saving me by taking herself away. . . . She could not be more wrong. Everything in my life depends on her being part of it.

When we first met, I was struck by her resemblance to her mother. But contrary to what many thought about my relationship with Gabrielle, we had a deep and affectionate friendship, nothing more. I loved her as an ally, and because she was our queen. I love her daughter in a completely different way. I love her because she has become something more to me. She has become my life.

"Come here," I say gently. "Sit down."

She shakes her head. "No. I . . . I can't stay."

"You want us to stop meeting." I have to say it because she will not.

"Yes."

"Because you think it is dangerous for me. Someone has told you something—my sister, perhaps." I cannot say Mimi's name in her presence, and vice versa. I cannot think of Mimi without thinking of the pain I am bringing her, and therefore choose the easier path: to not think of her at all. I am a coward.

"No."

"No?"

She walks over, closer to the fire, and addresses her words to the flames. "I can't meet you anymore, Jack, because I would be lying to myself for the reasons I'm here."

"And what is that reason?"

"That I love you."

"And that reason no longer exists, is that it?" My voice is light, playful. She is not a natural flirt; she is so serious always, my love, it amuses me a little. Of course she loves me. She is doing this precisely *because* she loves me.

"Yes."

"Another of my sister's ideas, isn't this? 'Tell Jack

you no longer love him. It is the only way to set him free.' As if I were a caged bird or a pet lion." I smile. Schuyler is so brave and full of courage, my darling. She will lose me to save me. She is ready to make that sacrifice, but I want her to know it is not necessary. I can fight for both of us, and I will.

"No." She looks at me, and her face is full of anguish. "No, that's not it."

It has been centuries since I have felt fear. I do not know fear. I do not have this weakness, and yet something in her face, in her voice—frightens me. This is no girlish deception, no halfhearted attempt. I marvel at my fear, at the novelty of it. It is like ice in my throat. It is lodged there; I cannot breathe. I cannot swallow.

Before I can say anything, she speaks, and the bluntness of her words strikes me as nothing has struck me before.

"I don't love you anymore because I haven't been honest with myself. And I haven't been honest with you. I love someone else. I always have."

A cruel joke. I want to laugh but I don't. I want to crumple to the ground but my pride will not let me. I have never heard these words before. I do not understand them. *Someone else? There is someone else?* This is a trick. Another deception. Another excuse Mimi has planted . . . Surely she cannot be . . . She is lying. . . .

Schuyler is telling the truth.

Of all the vampires in the world, I should know. I do not need the blood trial to find out. I can sense it—the truth is written all over her face. Her sadness. She is sad for me. She feels sorry—*for me*! I find her pity more disturbing than her words. It is ghastly and unimaginable.

How did she have time for someone else? I know our meetings were too few and far apart. But it was necessary, to keep her safe. If I'd had a choice—but I did not—we would have been together always. I lived for those moments when we were together, those few times in my life that I actually felt alive. Centuries I have slumbered until we met. And I had a plan for us. I had a future in mind. I wanted to share it with her and was waiting for the right moment. But the best-laid plans of mice and men . . .

I am not too proud to ask. "Who?"

"Oliver."

Her familiar. The human. I want to leave the room immediately so I can seek and destroy the mortal. He has no chance. She can see it.

"Please don't—don't harm him. I love him. I always

have. I just didn't want to admit it." For the first time this evening she reaches over and touches me. She puts her small hand—so tiny, really—on top of mine. I flinch, as if her fingers were engulfed in flames. *So this is pain. So this is wretchedness. So this is misery. I never knew.*

I have nothing to say. I can feel it—the truth. The truth of her love for him, it shines all over her face, and I can sense his presence on her very skin. Such is the way with the familiars—their blood brings us life, but they are not meant for us in this manner. I am sickened by jealousy and rage.

"Leave me." I am ashamed of the strangled cry that flies out before I can control myself.

"Jack . . . I . . ." She is standing by the doorway. I have hunted down the Croatan, I have endured the tortures of Hell, and yet I cannot find the strength to meet her eyes. I have to force myself to do so.

Her hand is on the door handle. "I'm sorry. I'm so sorry I lied to you all this time," she whispers.

"GO!" It is a roar from my throat. I cannot contain myself. I am transformed. I am Abbadon. Transformed into the demon I am. What does she see? What am I doing?

I see the fright in her eyes, taste her fear, revel in it,

and with brutal effort I catch myself before I get carried away. I am dangerous and flailing. It is I who needs to leave. I am gone before she can close the door.

From the street I watch as she leaves the building. I need to go back. I want to destroy that place. I want to destroy every memory it brings. I want it obliterated from the landscape. But when I return to the apartment, I am not alone.

Mimi is here.

When Schuyler left the building that evening, she thought she would feel at peace. Instead she felt more conflicted than before. The lie she told Jack had worked because she had wrapped it around the truth of her love for Oliver. Because it *was* a lie. She still loved Jack. She loved him so much that seeing him sitting there alone, in the dark, waiting patiently for her, made her love him even more.

She almost hadn't gone through with it. She didn't know what he would say or if she would be strong enough to see it through. It hurt her so much, seeing him look at her that way. She had never seen him so lost or confused.

I take it back! she'd wanted so much to say. *I take every-thing back. I love you. Let's go away. Just the two of us, together.*

But she'd had to do it. She had to let him go. Or give him a reason to let her go. It was the best choice for the two of them.

And it had worked.

She should feel relief—maybe even victorious.

So why did she feel so dead inside?

As if she had killed the best part of herself.

She walked slowly up to the avenue to catch a cab. She was moving back to Riverside Drive. She would not return to that town house on Fifth Avenue ever again.

Family Records:
Llewellyn

Due to the sensitive information contained in this file, most of it speculative in nature, this record is classified CONCLAVE LEVEL ONLY.

The Llewellyn family has risen to become one of the wealthiest and most powerful in the Coven. They amassed a great fortune by their monopoly of the New York and New Jersey seaports. A branch of the family moved to Houston during the oil boom during the late nineteenth century, and the majority of the family has been based there since.

BLISS LLEWELLYN

Azazel, the Darkling, Lupus Theliel, Angel of Love, Wolfsbane

Birth Name: Bliss Eugenia Llewellyn

Origin: November 9, 1991, Houston, Texas

Known Past Lives: Margaret Stanford (Newport), Mary Brewster (Plymouth), Giulia de Medici (Florence)

Bondmate: Unclear. Bliss has no heavenly past, but she does adhere to the cycles and the earliest record of her existence is {DATE REDACTED}.

Assigned Human Conduit: None

List of Human Familiars: Morgan Shriver (2007)

Physical Characteristiscs:

    Hair: Red

    Eyes: Green

    Height: 5'11"

It is the Repository's belief that Bliss Llewellyn is Gabrielle's first trueborn daughter, born from a union with Lucifer in {DATE REDACTED}. Bliss was believed to have been destroyed by the Regis upon her birth in {DATE REDACTED}. The Repository is still piecing together its information, which has not yet been verified, but it appears that the child survived through a betrayal by {NAME REDACTED—FL}. We are also tentatively able to conclude, given the information gleaned from various sources, that for centuries Allegra never had any knowledge of her child's existence.

The House of Records lists Bliss Llewellyn as carrying the spirit of the angel Yura, an angel of the Light. Yet a cross-reference on the history of the angel Yura revealed that Yura also appears on the List of the Finished, for whom reincarnation is no longer possible.

It is the Venators' belief that Forsyth Llewellyn, recently revealed to be yet another traitor Silver Blood on the conclave, has consistently used his elevated status to tamper with the birth record of Allegra's firstborn daughter, allowing him to call up her spirit in every incarnation and foster her in his home while keeping her true identity a secret. However, commendable work by our Repository scribes have brought forward the original birth record for Bliss Llewellyn for this cycle which was signed by then-Regent Nan Cutler. In this record, it lists her spirit as Azazel, angel of the dark, which we are now assuming is Bliss's the true name and one that was given to her by her father, the Morningstar.

Bliss grew up in Houston, Texas, and arrived at Duchesne her sophomore year. Texas Committee regional reports indicate that Bliss had a fierce and fearless personality, and was famous as the only cheerleader in the state who could execute a tumbling leap off the top of a fifty-person pyramid. She moved to New York when her father won the vacant senate seat, along with her stepmother and her younger half sister. It is the Venator's belief that BobiAnne Llewellyn was Bliss's birth mother in this cycle, a fact that was kept from Bliss for reasons that are still unverified.

A few months after moving to the city, Bliss was discovered during a Farnsworth scouting session at the school, and soon launched a very successful modeling career. Until recently, she was the face of several jeans campaigns, and her photographs were splashed across the billboards of Times Square and SoHo. Duchesne intern reports state that Bliss's early friendship with Mimi Force has since cooled and that she gravitated toward a friendship with Schuyler Van Alen, Oliver Hazard-Perry, and Dylan Ward.

Her rocky and ultimately tragic romance with Dylan Ward began with a chance meeting in an alley behind several nightclubs. He was her date to the fall Informals, and our sources suggest that she had planned to make him her human familiar (not knowing he was also a Blue

Blood), until he disappeared after Aggie Carondolet's death. (See Dylan Ward file for more information.)

From the late Warden Dupont's files, we found a note to Lawrence Van Alen that was never delivered:

Maggie Stanford was a sixteen-year-old Blue Blood who disappeared from the home of Admiral and Mrs. Thomas Vanderbilt during the 1870 Patrician Ball; foul play was suspected. Miss Stanford was the daughter of Mrs. and Mr. Tiberius Stanford of Newport, Rhode Island, the founder of Stanford Oil. Maggie was engaged at the time of her disappearance to Alfred, Lord Burlington, Earl of Devonshire.

Maggie was a patient at St. Dymphna Asylum, in Newport, for suicidal tendencies, delusions, and nightmares. The Red Blood doctors thought she was schizophrenic, but it is my belief that her symptoms were a sign of Corruption. Maggie tried to kill herself by drowning, but failed.

Lawrence: I think this is the clue. I think Maggie was Allegra's missing girl—

*Please come see me as soon as you are able
to come to the Repository.*

The Committee notes that this document was dated
the day of the Silver Blood attack that killed Warden
Dupont.

From Dr. Patricia Hazard's examination files on Bliss Llewellyn:

—Patient reports having blackouts and
nightmares since Transformation.
—Patient sees a crimson-eyed beast and a man
in a white suit who calls her "daughter."
—Patient's parents have been told of situation.
Senator Llwellyn promises to look into it.
—So far, no update from Senator Llewellyn
on patient's mental health.

Reprinted from a journal found in the Llewellyn's storage unit:

Venators report it is Bliss Llwellyn's handwriting, but
again, this is still unverified.

*Oh god, oh god, oh god. What can I do?
He's in me. Father. Visitor. I'm part*

of him. I can't get rid of him — he's in my mind, he can hear everything and he takes over — during the blackouts — that's what I've come to understand — I am him. He is me. I did it — I killed Dylan and so many others. I want to die. I am dead already. He'll come back soon — I have to go — he can't find out I can . . .

It is the Repository's conclusion that Bliss believed her "visitor" and the "father" she speaks of was none other than Lucifer, the Dark Prince himself. If so, it would explain why every trace of her birth was extinguished/manipulated in the House of Records.

During the attack at the Cathedral (for more information see Repository Record #404: *The Van Alen Legacy*), an eyewitness reports that Bliss took a blade from her bouquet, a "shard of glass that shone like gold fire" and plunged it into her chest. It is our belief that this was in fact the archangel Michael's sword, which has been missing for over a year. Bliss disappeared from view and has not been seen since; however, the Venators believe that she is still alive.

From the Venator report upon the visit to a studio apartment leased to one Jane Murray, who has since disappeared:

All signs point to a visit by Gabrielle. It is our belief that Allegra, once awakened, acknowledged Bliss as her own and gave her a new name: Lupus Theliel, Wolfsbane. The glom memory shows that while there were definitely three people in the room, only two were vampires; the other glom signature is distinctly human. We were also able to piece together a message that we believe was from Gabrielle: Find the Hounds of Hell. The demon fighters. Bring them back to the fold.

Bliss Llewellyn is a puzzle. She should never have been born, and her survival is a mystery. Lawrence Van Alen believed that Allegra's firstborn would be the death of the Blue Bloods, which is why he called for her destruction upon her birth. It remains to be seen whether Lawrence will be proven right in this matter.

Current Status: Missing. Location unknown. Believed to be searching for the "Hounds of Hell."

FORSYTH LLEWELLYN

Malakai, the Steward

Birth Name: Augustus Forsyth Llewellyn

Origin: November 14, 1959, New York, New York

Known Past Lives: Tiberius Stanford (Newport),
William Brewster (Plymouth), Duc Patrizio de Medici
(Florence), Naevius Macro (Rome)

Bondmate: BobiAnne Llewellyn

Assigned Human Conduit: Loel Salomon (recused
from service, 1981)

List of Human Familiars: Tierney Scott
(1973–1977), Evelyn Smith (1978–1983), Glory
Cason-Thrash (1985–1987), Samantha King
(1986–1992), Margot Pearson (1993–1999), Ashley
Wells (1998–2002)

Physical Characteristics:
　　Hair: Brown, speckled with gray
　　Eyes: Brown
　　Height: 5'10"

Forsyth Llewellyn was once one of Charles Force's most
trusted allies in the Conclave, but recent events have since
revealed that far from being an ally, Forsyth was most
likely Charles's greatest living adversary and a traitor to
the community. Forsyth grew up in Manhattan but soon

joined the family oil business in Houston, Texas. He moved back to New York when he won a vacant senate seat, an action prohibited by the Code of the Vampires, which states that Blue Bloods should not take political office. (It must be noted that the rule against entering Red Blood politics has always been weakly enforced, if at all, and through the centuries many Blue Bloods have held positions of authority in the human world.)

Forsyth Llewellyn has been revealed as a Silver Blood traitor, entrusted with the destruction of Allegra and Lucifer's firstborn child in {DATE REDACTED}. It is the Venators' belief that he let the child live in order to facilitate Lucifer's return. During his cycle as Tiberius Stanford, he supposedly died of grief shortly after his daughter Maggie went missing. However, the Repository files indicate he never showed Maggie very much affection and most likely was using grief to cover his fear at the repercussions from his true master had Maggie (Bliss) been able to destroy herself.

At the urging of Cordelia Van Alen, he also took the spirit of the Watcher, the Pistis Sophia, as his second daughter, Jordan. Cordelia suspected that Silver Blood treachery was afoot, and that one of the oldest families in the Conclave was working in league with our sworn enemies and possibly the Dark Prince himself. Little did she know that she was entrusting the traitor. . . .

The Repository now believes that, along with fellow Silver Blood traitor Nan Cutler, Forsyth arranged for Jordan to be taken by the Croatan. From his position in the Conclave he sent the Venators on a wild goose chase after her—sending those who could have unmasked him as far away as possible. After the murder of Lawrence Van Alen and the disappearance of Charles Force, Forsyth tried to instate himself as Regis. Only a lone objection from Mimi Force kept the vote from being unanimous.

He arranged for the bonding ceremony between the Force twins to take place so that the Silver Bloods could stage an attack at St. John the Divine, which we now believe he had guessed was the true location of the Gate of Time. If not for the remarkable sacrifice and bravery of Venator Martin, the Silver Bloods might have been able to open one of the Gates of Hell and let loose Abomination upon the world again, as during the Battle of Rome. Forsyth disappeared soon after the attack, and has not been seen since.

Current Status: Missing. Location unknown.

BOBIANNE LLEWELLYN

Andela, of the Dawn

Birth Name: Roberta Shepherd Prescott, known as "BobiAnne"

Origin: December 18, 1973, Houston, Texas

Known Past Lives: Dorothea Stanford (Newport), May Brewster (Plymouth), Antonia de Medici (Florence), Eunia Macro (Rome)

Bondmate: Forsyth Llewellyn

Assigned Human Conduit: None

List of Human Familiars: John-Boy Rogers (1991–1993), George Walton (1995–1997), Billy Busch (1998–2001), Richard Carter (2001–2006)

Physical Characteristics:
  Hair: Dyed blond
  Eyes: Brown
  Height: 5'9"

Described by Cordelia Van Alen as a prime example of the "downwardly aspirational" actions of the current incarnation of Blue Bloods, BobiAnne was known to be a superficial, silly, and ridiculous social climber; a tacky caricature who never quite fit in with the New York upper crust.

The much younger wife of Forsyth Llewellyn is referred to in all reports as Bliss's stepmother; however, there is no record of Forsyth's prior marriage, and a recently discovered copy of Bliss's birth certificate lists her birth mother as "R.P." the initials for Roberta Prescott. It is the Repository's conclusion that BobiAnne was Bliss's birth mother for her current incarnation but allowed the child to believe she was her stepmother, as Bliss had shown hostility toward her in prior life cycles. As Dorothea Stanford, she reportedly became mentally unbalanced after her daughter's disappearance, which we now believe was due to her fear that Maggie's true identity would be revealed to the Coven. Dorothea was convinced that her friends and neighbors were keeping the truth of her daughter's whereabouts from her.

She was also Jordan's birth mother. By all accounts, she barely tolerated the child, for reasons that have now become clear. The Venators believe that, like her husband, BobiAnne was a Silver Blood traitor, and feared that the Pistis Sophia would expose the couple for what they were: agents of the Prince of Darkness, foster parents to his secret heir. She perished during the massacre in Rio, a victim of her own nefarious schemes.

Forsyth Llewellyn was never the same after her death. As for New York and Texan society, they survived.

> **Current Status:** Finished. Slain during the Silver Blood attack in Rio.

JORDAN LLEWELLYN

Pistis Sophia, Elder of Elders, the Watcher
Birth Name: Jordan Grace Llewellyn
Origin: January 1, 1994, Houston, Texas
Known Former Aliases: Julia Livilla (Rome)
Current Alias: Jane Murray
Bondmate: None. The Pistis Sophia is a virgin incarnate and has no bondmate.
Physical Characteristics:
   Hair: As Jordan Llewellyn, brown
   As Jane Murray, red
   Eyes: As Jordan Llewellyn, green
   As Jane Murray, blue
   Height: As Jordan Llewellyn, 4'10"
   As Jane Murray, 5'5"

Jordan Llewellyn's true identity—the spirit of the Pistis Sophia, the Watcher—was known to only very few members of the Conclave: Cordelia Van Alen, who called for her rebirth; Forsyth Llewellyn, who fostered her and accepted her into his family; and the Regis, Charles Force, who finally gave his permission to the House of Records to call up the Sophia after Cordelia petitioned for it once too often.

The Watcher is an ancient soul born into full consciousness, with command of her memories and the ability to see the future. The Blue Bloods believe her wisdom will keep vigilance against Lucifer's return, but she has slumbered for thousands of years. She came to her position during the days of Rome, when she was then called Julia Livilla and sister to the emperor Caligula. She was the first who recognized Lucifer in him and joined forces with her sister Agrippina in a failed assassination attempt.

Michael released her spirit from the blood and freed her from having to adhere to the cycles of Expression. As the Pistis Sophia, in Rome she predicted the breaking of the bond between Michael and Gabrielle and prophesied that Gabrielle's daughter would be the salvation of the vampires.

As Jordan Llewellyn, the Sophia was a slightly awkward, short, and heavy girl, homely in contrast to her sister. At school she excelled in mathematics and science, and had a small group of friends. Family reports show that she followed Bliss around everywhere as a child, and, given Bliss's extraordinary origin, it is safe to conclude that Jordan knew exactly with whom she was dealing and was simply biding her time. Yet those who knew the sisters well reported that they were very close and shared an affectionate bond, which might explain why Jordan waited several years before making the decision to strike.

The Venators believe that on the night of her abduction in Rio, the Watcher in Jordan finally took action. She tried to kill Bliss in her sleep, but was discovered at the last moment by Forsyth and BobiAnne. From Venator Martin's subsequent investigation, it appears that Jordan was held captive by Silver Bloods at Lucifer's command for a year, in an attempt to extract information on the Order of the Seven. When it appeared she would never give them this information, they killed her. Or so they thought. The Watcher is capable of changing physical shells, and as Jordan died, Sophia found a new host in Jane Murray, a forty-year-old history teacher who had been hit by a bus while traveling in South America.

As Jane Murray, Sophia is now a sturdy, apple-cheeked woman with bright red hair and a ruddy Irish complexion. In 2009, she joined the staff of Duchesne as a history teacher. School reports from Duchesne indicate she was incredibly popular; her seminar, Ancient Civilizations, was continually overenrolled.

The Venators have pieced together this information from Jane Murray's ransacked apartment, and we can only conclude that the Watcher is with Bliss Llewellyn, wherever she may be.

> **Current Status:** Missing. Believed to be in the company of Bliss Llewellyn.

Author's Note: I am in the process of writing the first book in the Wolf Pact series. The idea for Wolf Pact came very early to me, when I was writing the major outline for the Blue Bloods books, and once the story expanded, the wolves seemed to merit a series of their own. The following is a sneak peek at the first book. The series follows the continuing story of Bliss Llewellyn as she sets off to find the Hounds of Hell.

WOLF PACT

he shadows made everything look larger, and smell worse. Styrofoam platters and massive rolls of waxed paper were stacked on the counters. Hooks from empty meat racks hung from the ceiling, their crooked silhouettes looking even more ominous in the moonlight. Tacked on the brick walls were charts mapping animal parts. Shoulder. Chuck. Loin. Near the entrance were two large glass counters full of steaks and chops wrapped in cellophane.

DICKINSON AREA
PUBLIC LIBRARY

Bliss Llewellyn took a deep breath and held it for as long as she could, willing her tense muscles to relax. She had tracked the beast inside the butcher shop, had watched its arched, furry body slink in through the back door. This was it. She'd been in Hunting Valley for three days now, and had combed every inch of it, which wasn't too hard, really. It was barely a town—the downtown area consisting of one honky-tonk bar and several boarded-up storefronts. It was the kind of place most people left as soon as they had the means; the kind of place for those left behind.

Bliss crept as quietly as she could across the wet stone floor. This was the end of her chase. Everything she had done so far had led to this moment. The beast was lurking somewhere within the darkness, waiting. She would have to be quick. She had seen the carnage it had left in the woods, had followed the trail, and now she was at its end. *Tame the hounds*, her mother had told her. *Bring them back to the fold.* She would have to bring it to heel, somehow. Her eyes caught a flicker of light in the distance. In the back of the room she noticed the door to the meat locker was open, revealing a carcass swaying like an inverted pendulum. So that was why her surroundings smelled of blood.

She closed her eyes so she could hear. *Concentrate.* She pinched her nose. The smell was distracting. When the Visitor had been her only contact to the outside (or was that inside?) world, she found she could listen better if she closed her eyes and withdrew from her other senses. She was human now, with human limitations. She could no longer listen to a conversation conducted fifty feet away; she could no longer lift objects five times her body weight; she could no longer do any of the things she had taken for granted when her blood was blue.

But even if she was only human, she was used to the dark. The Visitor had taught her that. She heard a clock tick, the sound of a hook grinding against a chain, heard the soft click of claws against the concrete—the beast, stirring . . . and then there, barely perceptible, was the sound of breathing. There was someone else in the room, someone other than the creature. But where? And who?

The horrible clicking grew louder, and Bliss heard a snarl, deep and primeval and vicious, and then the sound of breathing became louder, more desperate— suddenly a scream from beyond the doorway. Bliss leapt from her hiding place and ran toward it.

Clang!

A knife fell to the floor. She swiveled in its direction, then stopped. The knife was a ruse, a distraction. The beast was behind her now; it was trying to steer her away from the door. She could see it watching her from the shadows, its crimson eyes staring at her balefully. Did it think she was stupid? She might not have her vampire abilities anymore, but that didn't mean she was completely useless. She was still fast. She was still coordinated. She had the speed and skill of an athlete.

The beast snorted and raked its claws across the concrete. It was angry and getting ready to jump. Bliss figured it was now or never. She pushed her way toward the open door, clambering onto a table and spraying a dozen knives across the room. The beast leapt but she was faster, and when she reached the oversized steel door, she grabbed the handle and, using its weight as a pivot, swung around so that she pulled it closed behind her. The freezer slammed shut with a thick, wet sucking sound that made her wonder if this had been a good idea. How much air was in here? No time to worry about that now. She grabbed a knife hanging on the wall and jammed the lock closed.

She could hear the creature throwing its weight against the bolted door, making the archway shake. It was larger and more dangerous than she had thought. Tame the hounds? She would be lucky if she got out of here alive.

She looked around. There were a dozen or so carcasses hanging from the ceiling. The air was rancid, metallic. She pushed her way through the animal corpses to the back of the freezer, toward the sound of ragged breathing.

On the floor of the meat locker lay a boy, no older than she was, chained to the back wall. Next to him were a cutting board and a band saw. A meat hook swung above his head, crusted with blood and rust. The tiled walls were splattered a deep shade of scarlet. The boy's skin was blue, his hair caked with filth . . . there were ugly red marks around his wrists and neck, where he was bound with heavy iron shackles. Dear God, what was going on here? Bliss wondered, her stomach churning. . . .

The beast couldn't have done this alone. There was something else going on. Bliss shivered, goose bumps appearing on her skin. Now that she wasn't a vampire, her body did not control its temperature as well as it used to. But was it fear or the cold that had caused the rows of tiny bumps? For the first time in her journey, Bliss wondered if she was in over her head.

She bent down to touch the boy's face. It was still warm at least. She placed a tender hand on his bony shoulder. "You are going to be okay," she told him, and wondered if she was also consoling herself.

"Yes, but you're not." His eyes came alive, and before Bliss could blink, the boy had wrapped his fist around her neck and pinned her to the floor, locking his knees against her waist and keeping her arms away from her body. His shackles, Bliss could see now, had not been locked.

"Who are you?" she asked, spitting out the words with difficulty, recoiling from the boy's grip around her neck. She wondered if she could reach into her jean pocket to stab him with the hidden blade she always kept there.

"I think the correct question is, who are you? You're in our territory." His voice was low and musical, friendly.

"I don't know what you mean."

"We don't like the likes of you here. You smell like the glom," he said, and she knew he meant that she was not quite human; that somehow, he could sense her formerly immortal stature, when she had once been an angel of fire.

"You know about the glom?" Bliss asked.

The boy laughed. "We hunt *in* the glom. We are the *Abyssus Praetorium*."

Bliss startled. She'd heard the term before. The Guards of the Abyss. Also known as the Praetorian Guard. An image flashed in her mind. She saw the Visitor—Lucifer—her father—standing inside an elaborate palace, surrounded by magnificent columns of gold. A cast of thousands was gathered around his court. Was this Rome? Or ancient Egypt? She couldn't tell. Lucifer stood at the top of a marble staircase, looking down at a creature of exquisite beauty. It was a man, but he was taller than a human male, with a certain otherworldly magnificence, wild-eyed and ferocious.

The image did not come from her memory but from Lucifer's. When she had been captive to his spirit, when he had taken over her soul, fragments of his memories had drifted into her consciousness. Triggered by random events, memories she'd never had would suddenly pop into her mind. So. The Visitor knew these creatures. She closed her eyes to recall the scene once more. She could hear Lucifer speak. The language was unfamiliar, its words harsh and convoluted, but she knew she could speak them as if they were her own.

"آزادی من!" *Release me*, she cried, just as the boy's hand tightened on her throat. The room froze and from the other side of the door, the beast howled. Then the boy's grip eased and he fell away, staring at her in amazement and confusion, as if he could not quite understand why he had let her go.

She was as she shocked as he was, but she didn't have any time to lose. In one fluid motion, Bliss rolled away and bolted from the room, catching her balance before she slipped in a puddle of blood. She wrenched the knife from the freezer door and ran through the doorway and back out into the shop.

What just happened? She had tracked the creature for weeks, and now suddenly it seemed that *she* was the one who was being pursued. Had Lucifer sent the creature to lure her here? Was he somehow able to reach her once more? Was the boy working for him? How could Allegra have led her to this hellhole? Was everything she had been told and everything she believed nothing but a lie?

Bliss pushed against the front door, surprised to find it was locked. She had purposefully left it open when she'd entered. Who had locked it? She kicked at the jamb, splitting it in two and throwing glass out onto the street. She flung the door open and skidded out onto the sidewalk. Tiny shards of glass dug into her shoes as she stumbled across the pavement toward her car. She heard the slap of running footsteps behind her, but she didn't turn. Grabbing the keys out of her pocket, she wrestled the door open, slid into the driver's seat, and fired the engine. She looked ahead of her, and then behind. She was parked in from both sides, the other cars mere inches away from hers. There was no way she could get out without doing damage to either vehicle, or her own. It was obviously a trap. She'd just have to smash her way out. She floored the gas pedal, and slammed into the car in front of her. It moved, but barely.

She slammed on the gas again, this time throwing the car into reverse, and plowed directly into the car behind her, causing a sickening crunch of metal against metal as the back end of her car crunched like an accordion and her taillights exploded in a shower of plastic and dust. She threw the car back into drive and pancaked the rear bumper of the car in front of her. Her own car popped up on the curb—that was more like it—allowing her to twist her way out from between the two cars that had trapped her in front of the butcher shop.

Sweat dripped from her forehead and into her eyes. She blinked, feeling dizzy. She was human now, and despite her strength, she would have to get used to her new limitations. She hit the gas again and powered forward, turning the wheel, speeding wildly down the street. The windshield had cracked, making it hard to see, and she immediately crashed into a telephone pole. The windshield caved in, and the car swung sideways as it plowed into the curb. Bliss was thrown backward against the headrest. What had she done? She had gone from escape to disaster in only a few seconds. The car was demolished. She hit the gas again, but nothing happened. She tried reverse, but the engine was dead.

Then a loud thump hit the top of the car, and the roof caved in slightly. She saw a pair of boots descend from the top of the car to the hood, followed by four hairy paws. So that's where the beast had gone. She could see it more clearly now—its silver fur, its crimson eyes. They settled in front of her, the boy and the wolf, both of them crouched on their haunches, nimble as acrobats as they stared at her through the broken windshield.

Behind them, she could see others, a group of kids slowly circling the car. How many were they? Three?

Four? More? She caught a glimpse of a fierce-looking girl with wild green hair and tattoos, and several boys who looked dark and menacing. Someone was trying to pry open the rear passenger-side door. The handle rattled, but all of the doors had been smashed shut. Bliss took a deep breath and waited. "What do you want from me?"

The boy smiled. "I want you to calm down before you hurt yourself, Bliss."

He knows my name. How does he know my name?

"I'm Lawson, by the way."

She nodded, but her attention was elsewhere. The wolf had pushed forward, its teeth inches from her face. Spit oozed from its mouth; the odor was unbearable. Lawson coaxed the creature's head away, so it backed off from Bliss with a whimper.

"Come on now, Scooby, lay off," he said, giving the creature an affectionate shake.

One of the kids standing near the car—a little girl, Bliss could now see—she couldn't have been more than eleven—tossed over a dog biscuit. The wolf caught the treat in midair and wandered away from the car, tail wagging.

"Scooby?" The wolf was his pet. Bliss tried not to

look too incredulous. When her mother had sent her on this quest, she had imagined the Hounds of Hell as supernatural creatures. Beasts that were half human and half animal, something from nightmares and horror movies. Hellhound, werewolf . . . same thing, right?

"Is that what you thought? That we *turned* into them? At the sight of a full moon?" Lawson smirked. How did he know what she was thinking? It was as if he had heard every word. Venators could do that, of course, but she could tell he wasn't a vampire. What was he then? And who was "we"? That group of kids around the car? Were they with him? They had to be.

Lawson threw back his head and howled. He pulled at his shirt collar in an imitation of an uncontrollable dramatic transformation. "You're not serious are you?" he asked, looking a bit insulted. "I mean, you know there's no such thing as werewolves, right? They were invented by some desperate screenwriter in the 1940s. We noticed you'd been following Scooby for a while and thought it was high time we finally met. Sorry if what we arranged was a little crude. The boys have a sick sense of humor. Comes from living in the wild, I guess."

Bliss didn't know what to say. Lawson was awfully chatty for someone who, moments ago, seemed to mean her quite a bit of harm. Her neck still pinched where he had held her.

"Sorry about your car, by the way; although you didn't need to overreact so much. Anyway, we'll get you another one. Or Gorg could fix it. Whatever you'd like. But we need to talk about what happened in there. How do you know our language? Nothing like that has ever happened to us before. We thought we knew every Praetorian in the district." He studied her face closely and then plucked a handkerchief from his pocket and dabbed her cheek with it. "Best we get you inside and clean up this mess before the police arrive. We don't like to attract attention. This town might look dead, but I assure you, the small-minded sheriff is very much alive."

He hopped off the car and easily lifted open the damaged driver's side door. The metal was bent and twisted, but he hadn't even broken a sweat. He wasn't as frail as he had looked earlier, nor as skinny. Bliss wondered if he had been able to adjust his presence somehow. He was quite tall and muscular. Whatever he was—or any of his friends, for that matter—he was not quite human. But neither did he resemble the exquisite monsters from Lucifer's memory. In any event, he was as much a mystery to her as she was to him.

"Coming?" he asked, waiting for her to step out of the car.

Bliss winced. In the heat of the moment, she hadn't felt the pain. But now it was unbearable. "I think both my legs are broken."

"Oh god, now I'm really sorry Malcolm talked me into such a stupid stunt. Here," he said, bending down so that she could put her arms around his neck.

Her legs dangled uselessly as he carried her back to the butcher shop, and she took the opportunity to study him in more detail. He must have wiped the gunk from his hair, because under the glow of the streetlight, Bliss could see that it was actually a lovely deep chestnut color. He had sharp, fine features, wide blue eyes and an Irish nose, a square jaw and a strong forehead. He wasn't frail and sickly at all, but young, virile, and very handsome.

After months of searching, Bliss felt oddly safe in his strong arms, and wondered exactly who or what she had found in Hunting Valley.

Behind them, his team was already clearing away every trace of the accident.

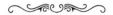

FAMILY RECORDS:
OFF-COVEN

While most, if not all, Blue Bloods families are registered with the Coven, there are a few who choose to live outside of Committee jurisdiction. These families and individuals are not affiliated with the Silver Blood threat, but neither do they help advance the Blue Bloods' core mission. They do not attend Committee meetings, are not active in Coven leadership, and for reasons of their own, prefer to live outside and apart form the community.

DYLAN WARD

Xathaneal, the Hidden One
Birth Name: Dylan Elliot Ward
Origin: May 5, 1992, Greenwich, Connecticut
Known Past Lives: Alfred, Lord Burlington, Earl of
Devonshire (Newport), William Bradford (Plymouth),
Paolo Ghiberti (Florence)
Bondmate: None
Assigned Human Conduit: None
List of Human Familiars: Unknown
Physical Characteristics:
    Hair: Black
    Eyes: Black
    Height: 5'9"

Very little is known of the Ward family since they chose
to live off-Coven at the beginning of the twentieth
century. The only member that has come to the
Committee's attention is Dylan, for his role in unmask-
ing the Silver Blood conspiracy.

Dylan enrolled at the Duchesne School his sophomore year, and the intern reports state that rumors began circulating from the very beginning that he had been
kicked out of every prep school on the Northeastern

Seaboard, fueled perhaps by his attitude (sullen, aloof, a perpetual scowl) and his purposefully grungy attire (beat-up leather jacket, dirty jeans). However, the truth is much more mundane. Dylan attended Greenwich elementary and middle schools, where he was an average student.

He found friendship with fellow misfits Schuyler Van Alen and Oliver Hazard-Perry, and a budding romance with Bliss Llewellyn, who was overheard saying, "Dylan's the kind of boy who broke the rules and let anything happen, and I like that about him."

The prime suspect of the murder of Aggie Carondolet, Dylan was being held by the Committee for questioning when he escaped and was believed to have attacked again, this time targeting Cordelia Van Alen. However, we now believe that far from being the perpetrator and suffering from Corruption, he was in fact yet another Silver Blood victim, whose memory had been egregiously tampered with, causing disorientation and incoherence. The Venators now believe that Bliss Llewellyn, under the influence of Lucifer, was the real perpetrator.

When Dylan reappeared in New York, he sought out Bliss, who turned him over to her cycle father. Forsyth Llewellyn immediately checked him into Transitions, the vampire rehabilitation center. He was checked out after only a few weeks, and his dead body was later found on Corcovado Mountain, next to the corpse of Lawrence Van Alen.

As a vampire with no bondmate, Xathaneal was free to choose a cycle mate among the Coven, and was continually drawn to Azazel (Bliss) over history. In 1870, as the eldest son of the Duke and Duchess of Devonshire, he was engaged to marry Maggie Stanford at the time of her disappearance. It is the Repository's belief that in other incarnations he was drawn to her as well. May Brewster became Goody Bradford, and Giulia de Medici was pledged to Paolo Ghiberti.

Current Status: Finished. Slain by Lawrence Van Alen in Rio.

(See *Revelations*: Repository Record #303 for more information on his death.)

Author's Note: This story takes place after the events in Blue Bloods *and before* Masquerade. *The story is not told from Dylan's point of view, but does shed a little more light on what happened to him.*

SHELTER ISLAND
Dylan's Story

t was the light that started it. Hannah woke up at three o'clock in the morning one cold February day and noticed that one of the old copper sconces along the wall was turned on, emitting a dim, barely perceptible halo. It flickered at first, then died, then abruptly came back to life again. At first she chalked it up to a faulty wire, or carelessness on her part—had she turned off the lights before bed? But when it happened again the next evening, and again two days later, she began to pay attention.

The fourth time, she was already awake when it happened. She felt around the nightstand for her glasses, put them on, then stared at the glowing bulb and frowned. She definitely remembered turning off the switch before going to bed. She watched as it slowly burned out, leaving the room dark once more. Then she went back to sleep.

Another girl would have been scared, but this was Hannah's third winter on Shelter Island and she was used to its "house noises" and assorted eccentricities. In the summer, the back screen door never stayed closed; it would bang over and over with the wind, or when someone walked in and out of the house—her mother's boyfriend, a neighbor, Hannah's friends whose parents had houses on the island and spent their summers there. No one ever locked their doors on Shelter Island. There was no crime (unless bike-stealing was considered a crime, and if your bike was gone, most likely someone just borrowed it to pedal down to the local market, and you would find it on your front doorstep the next day), and the last murder had been recorded sometime in the 1700s.

Hannah was fifteen years old, and her mother, Kate, was a bartender at The Good Shop, a crunchy, all-organic restaurant and bar that was only open three months out of the year, during the high season, when the island was *infested* (her mother's word) with city folk on vacation. The *summer people* (also her mother's words) and their money made living on the island possible for year-rounders like them. During the off-season, in the winter, there were so few people on the island it was akin to living in a ghost town.

But Hannah liked the winters, liked watching the ferry cross the icy river, how the quiet snow covered everything like a fairy blanket. She would walk alone on the windswept beach, where the slushy sound of her boots scuffing the damp sand was the only sound for miles. People always threatened to quit the island during the winter. They'd had enough of the brutal snowstorms that raged in the night, the wind howling like a crazed banshee against the windows. They complained of the loneliness, the isolation. Some people didn't like the sound of quiet, but Hannah reveled in it. Only then could she hear herself think.

Hannah and her mother had started out as summer people. Once upon a time, when her parents were still together, the family would vacation in one of the big Colonial mansions by the beach, near where the yachts docked by the Sunset Beach hotel. But things were different after the divorce. Hannah understood that their lives had been lessened by the split, that she and her mother were lesser people now, in some way. Objects of pity ever since her dad ran off with his art dealer.

Not that Hannah cared very much what other people thought. She liked the house they lived in, a comfortable, ramshackle Cape Cod with a wraparound porch and six bedrooms tucked away in its corners—one up in the attic, three on the ground floor, and two in the basement. There were antique nautical prints of the island and its surrounding waters, framed in the wood-paneled living room. The house belonged to a family who never used it, and the caretaker didn't mind renting it to a single mother.

At first, she and her mother had moved around the vast space like two marbles lost on a pinball table. But over time they adjusted and the house felt cozy and warm. Hannah never felt lonely or scared. She always felt safe.

Still, the next night, at three o'clock in the morning, when the lights blinked on and the door whooshed open with a bang, it startled Hannah and she sat up immediately, looking around. Where had the wind come from? The windows were all storm-proofed and she hadn't felt a draft. With a start, she noticed a shadow lingering by the doorway.

"Who's there?" she called out in a firm, no-nonsense

voice. It was the kind of voice she used when she worked as a cashier at the marked-up grocery store during the summers and the city folk complained about the price of arugula.

She wasn't scared. Just curious. What would cause the lights to blink on and off and the door to bang open like that?

"Nobody," someone answered.

Hannah turned around.

There was a boy sitting in the chair in the corner.

Hannah almost screamed. She had been expecting a cat, maybe a lost squirrel of some sort, but a boy? She was fast approaching her sweet-sixteen-and-never-been-kissed milestone. It was awful how some girls made such a big deal out of it, but even more awful that Hannah agreed with them.

"Who are you? What are you doing here?" Hannah said, trying to feel braver than she felt.

"This is my home," the boy said calmly. He was her age, she could tell, maybe a bit older. He had dark shaggy hair that fell in his eyes, and he was wearing torn jeans and a dirty T-shirt. He was very handsome, but he looked pensive and pained. There was an ugly cut on his neck.

Hannah pulled up the covers to her chin, if only to hide her pajamas, which were flannel and printed with pictures of sushi. How had he gotten into her room without her noticing? What did he want with her? Should she cry out? Let her mother know? That wound on his neck—it looked ravaged. Something awful had happened to him, and Hannah felt her skin prickle with goose bumps.

"Who are you?" the boy asked, suddenly turning the tables.

"I'm Hannah," she said in a small voice. Why had she told him her real name? Did it matter?

"Do you live here?"

"Yes."

"How strange," the boy said thoughtfully. "Well," he said, "nice meeting you, Hannah." Then he walked out of her room and closed the door. Soon after, the light blinked off.

Hannah lay in her bed, wide awake, for a very long time, her heart galloping in her chest. The next morning, she didn't tell her mom about the boy in her room. She convinced herself it was just a dream. That was it. She had just made him up. Especially the part about him looking like a younger Johnny Depp. She'd been wanting a boyfriend so much, she'd made one appear. Not that he would be her boyfriend. But if she was ever going to have a boyfriend, she would like him to look like that. Not that boys who looked like that ever looked at girls like her. Hannah knew what she looked like. Small. Average. Quiet. Her nicest feature were her eyes: seaglass green framed with lush dark lashes. But they were hidden behind her eyeglasses most of the time.

Her mother always accused her of having an overactive imagination, and maybe that was all this was. She had finally let the winter crazies get to her. It was all in her mind.

But then he returned the next evening, wandering into her room as if he belonged there. She gaped at him, too frightened to say a word, and he gave her a courtly bow before disappearing. The next night, she didn't fall asleep. Instead, she waited.

Three in the morning.

The lights blazed on. Was it just Hannah's imagination, or was the light actually growing stronger? The door banged. This time, Hannah was awake and had expected it. She saw the boy appear in front of her closet, materializing out of nowhere. She blinked her eyes, blood roaring in her ears, trying to fight the panic welling up inside. Whatever he was . . . he wasn't *human.*

"You again," she called, trying to feel brave.

He turned around. He was wearing the same clothes as the two nights prior. He gave her a sad, wistful smile. "Yes."

"Who are you? What are you?" she demanded.

"Me?" He looked puzzled for a moment, and then stretched his neck. She could see the wound just underneath his chin more clearly this time. Two punctures. Scabby and . . . blue. They were a deep indigo color, not the brownish-red she had been expecting. "I think I'm what you call a vampire."

"A vampire?" Hannah recoiled. If he were a ghost, it would be a different story. Hannah's aunt had told her all about ghosts—she had gone through a Wiccan phase, as well as a spirit-guide phase. Hannah wasn't afraid of ghosts. Ghosts couldn't harm you, unless it was a poltergeist. Ghosts were vapors, spectral images, maybe even just a trick of the light.

But vampires . . . there was a Shelter Island legend about a family of vampires who had terrorized the island a long time ago. Blood-sucking monsters, pale and undead, cold and clammy to the touch, creatures of the night that could turn into bats, or rats, or worse. She shivered and looked around the room, wondering how fast she could jump out of bed and out the door. If there was even time to escape, could you outrun a vampire?

"Don't worry, I'm not that kind of vampire," he said soothingly, as if he'd read her mind.

"What kind would that be?"

"Oh you know, chomping on people without warning. All that Dracula nonsense. Growing horns out of my head like your sad vampires on T.V." He shrugged. "For one thing, we're not ugly."

Hannah wanted to laugh but felt it would be rude. Her fright was slowly abating.

"Why are you here?"

"We live here," he said simply.

"No one lived here for years before us," Hannah said. "John Carter—the caretaker, he said it's been empty forever."

"Huh." The boy shrugged. He took the corner seat across from her bed.

Hannah glanced at him warily, wondering if she should let him get that close. If he was a vampire, he didn't look cold and clammy. He looked tired. Exhausted. There were dark circles under his eyes. He didn't look like a cold-blooded killer. But what did she know? Could she trust him? He had visited her twice already, after all. If he'd wanted to drain her blood, he could have at any time. There was something about him—he was almost too cute to be scared of.

"Why do you keep doing that?" she asked, when she found her voice.

"Oh, you mean the thing with the lights?"

She nodded.

"Dunno. For a long time, I couldn't do anything. I was sleeping in your closet but you didn't see me. Then I realized I could turn the lights on and off, on and off. But it was only when you started noticing that I began to feel more like myself."

"Why are you here?"

The boy closed his eyes. "I'm hiding from someone."

"Who?"

He closed his eyes harder, so that his face was a painful grimace. "Somebody bad. Somebody who wants me dead—No, worse than dead." He shuddered.

"If you're a vampire, aren't you already dead?" she asked in a practical tone. She felt herself relaxing. Why should she be scared of him when it was so obvious it was he who was frightened?

"No, not really. It's more like I've lived a long time. A long time," he murmured. "This is my house. I remember the fireplace downstairs. I put the plaque up myself." He must be talking about that dusty old plaque next to the fireplace, Hannah thought. But it was so old and dirty she had never thought to notice it before.

"Who's chasing you?" Hannah asked.

"It's compli—" but before the boy could finish, there was a rattle at the window. A thump, thump, thump, as if someone—or something—were throwing itself against it with all its might.

The boy jumped and vanished for a moment. He reappeared by the doorway, breathing fast and hard.

"What is that?" Hannah asked, her voice trembling.

"It's here. It found me," he said sharply, as if he were about to flee. And yet he remained where he was, his eyes fixed on the vibrating glass.

"Who?"

"The bad . . . thing . . ."

Hannah stood up and peered out the window. Outside was dark and peaceful. The trees, skeletal and bare of branches, stood still in the snowy field and against the frozen water. Moonlight cast the view in a cold, blue glow.

"I don't see any— Oh!" She stepped back as if she'd been stabbed. She had seen something. A presence. Crimson eyes and silver pupils. Staring at her from the dark. Outside the window, it was hovering. A dark mass. She could feel its rage, its violent desire. It wanted in, to consume, to feed.

Hannah . . . Hannah . . .

It knew her name.

Let me in . . . Let me in . . .

The words had a hypnotic effect. She moved toward the window and began to lift the latch.

"STOP!"

She turned. The boy stood at the doorway, a tense, frantic look on his face.

"Don't," he said. "That's what it wants you to do. Invite it inside. As long as you keep that window closed, it can't come in. And I'm safe."

"What *is* it?" Hannah asked, her heart pounding hard in her chest. She took her hand away from the window but kept her eyes on the view outside. There was nothing there anymore, but she could sense its presence. It was near.

"A vampire too. Like me, but different. It's . . . insane," he said. "It feeds on its own kind."

"A vampire that hunts vampires?"

The boy nodded. "I know it sounds ridiculous . . ."

"Did it . . . do that to you?" she said, crossing to him and brushing her fingers against the scabs on his neck. They felt rough to touch. She felt sorry for him.

"Yes."

"But you're all right?"

"I think so." He hung his head. "I hope so."

"How were you able to come inside? No one invited you," she asked.

"You're right. But I didn't need an invitation. The door was open. But so many doors were open on all the houses, and I couldn't enter any of them but this one. Which made me think that I'd found it. My family's house."

Hannah nodded. That made sense. Of course he would be welcome in his own home.

The rattling stopped. The boy sighed. "It's gone for now. But it will be back."

He looked so relieved that her heart went out to him.

"What do you need me to do?" she asked. She wasn't

scared anymore. Her mother always said Hannah had a head for emergencies. She was a stoic, dependable girl. More likely to plant a stake in the heart of a monster than scream for rescue from the railroad tracks. "How can I help?"

He raised an eyebrow and looked at her with respect. "I need to get away. I can't stay here forever. I need to go. I need to warn the others. Tell them what happened to me. That the danger is growing." He sagged against the wall. "What I ask you to do might hurt a bit, and I don't want to ask unless it's freely given."

"Blood, isn't it? You need blood. You're weak," Hannah said. "You need my blood."

"Yes." The shadows cast his face in sharp angles, and Hannah could see the deep hollows in his cheeks. His sallow complexion. So perhaps some of the vampire legends were true.

"But won't I turn into . . . ?"

"No." He shook his head. "It doesn't work that way. No one can make a vampire. We were born like this. Cursed. You will be fine—tired and a little sleepy, maybe, but fine."

Hannah gulped. "Is it the only way?" She didn't much like how that sounded. He would have to bite her.

Suck her blood. She felt nauseous just thinking about it, but strangely excited as well.

The boy nodded slowly. "I understand if you don't want to. It's not something that most people would like to do."

"Can I think about it?" she asked.

"Of course," he said.

Then he disappeared.

The next night, when he returned, he looked even sicker than he had before, as if he were fading—deteriorating right before her eyes. His cheekbones were so sharp and his skin stretched so tight, Hannah thought she could see the outline of his skull. He looks half dead, she thought, and wondered if someone who *was* undead could *look* half dead.

"You're not half wrong." He smiled.

"You read minds as well." It was a statement, not a question.

"I can when I want to—but I didn't even have to—I can tell from the way you're looking at me. I look that bad, huh?"

She nodded. "I'm sorry."

"I'm so stupid," the boy said, putting clenched fists

up to his eyes as if he were trying to block out a horrible memory. "I should have known from the beginning—I'm so very stupid. . . ." He removed his fists from his face and looked down at his dirty fingernails.

"What are you talking about?" she asked.

The boy continued to rant in a furious whisper. "I should have known it was her. I did know, but I forgot. . . . I think she used me or something . . . inside her did . . . everything's so muddled in my mind . . . I mean, I remember what happened but sometimes I can't believe it did happen . . . and I feel like *I'm* the one who should be out there. Sometimes I feel like I *am* out there."

He wasn't making any sense, and Hannah was starting to feel as confused as he sounded. "Who's she?" But he didn't have to say it. This time, it was written all over the anguish on his face. Hannah felt a quick stab of jealousy. There was another girl involved. There always was. You didn't get to look like him—weary and handsome, with those sad black eyes—and not have some kind of girlfriend baggage.

"She was very special to me," he murmured. "But I think I'm going to have to get back . . . so I can. God. So I can kill her." Then he broke down into gasping, choking sobs. "I have to . . . but I don't know if I'll be able to. . . . I might just let it have me. . . . It would be easier in a way."

Hannah got up from her bed and embraced him. She was not a touchy-feely kind of person but she wanted to do something to make him feel better. When her parents first separated, she was a zombie, an empty shell, devoid of feeling, but aching with a great and furious need for comfort. Her mother had tried to help, to reach out, but Hannah had resisted accepting succor from the person who was partly to blame for her misery. After all, maybe if her mother hadn't been such a hard person to live with, her father would never have left her for Delphine, the Temptress Art Dealer. Who knew.

But whatever sorrow the divorce had brought to her life paled in comparison to what this boy was going through. He radiated fear, trembling in her arms. She didn't really understand what he was telling her, but she could tell that he was running out of time.

Something thumped on the window hard, making them jump away from each other. Hannah took a sharp breath. The glass vibrated, but held and didn't shatter. That vampire thing was back. It was out there. It was close. It wanted to feed.

And so did he.

The boy needed her blood, the strength and life force within it. He needed her to survive. He would die without her. Maybe not the kind of death humans experienced, but an emptiness nonetheless. A defeat. He would give himself up. He was growing weaker and weaker, and one day he wouldn't be able to resist the monster's call. He would walk out to meet his doom.

All he needed was to sink his fangs into her skin and drink her blood.

Hannah felt a shiver of revulsion at the thought. He was a monster, too. There was a monster in her bedroom. She moved away from him, her eyes wide and frightened as if seeing him for the first time. A stranger. A dirty, incoherent, and unwelcome stranger.

She shook her head. "I'm sorry, but I can't help you. I think you should leave now."

"It's all right," he said mournfully. "I didn't expect you to. It's a lot to ask."

The light blinked off, and he was gone.

Hannah's mother got up early the next morning to make her breakfast. Banana pancakes with maple syrup that came from the can with the Canadian flag on it.

Hannah twirled the syrup around before taking a bite.

"Not hungry?" Kate asked. Kate had been the kind of person who ordered the housekeeper to make breakfast, who had made lists on Post-it notes, a litany of orders for the staff to take care of for the day. Hannah had never seen her mother cook anything aside from the random scrambled egg or the rare serving of pasta. Kate made one dish and made it well—spaghetti with meatballs. Now she cooked and cleaned, and her hands were dry and cracked from wiping down the bar at work. In the winter, Kate was a sous-chef at the attached restaurant, chopping carrots and boning chickens.

"Not really." Hannah shook her head. She had never wished for the kind of relationship with her mother that meant they could talk about boys and crushes; she was almost glad that her mother didn't jibe with the current intense befriending of her children. Kate was Mom. Hannah was Daughter. There was no girlfriend gossip between them, and that had suited them both fine.

"You look tired, hon. Please don't read with that dim light up there. It'll ruin your eyes."

"My eyes are already ruined."

Her mom drove her to the school, a few blocks away. Hannah trudged in the snow. The whole day she thought about him. She remembered his words, his desperation to get away from the creature in the night that was hunting him. How alone he had looked. How scared. He looked like how she had felt when her father had told her he was leaving them, and her mother had had no one to turn to.

That evening, before going to bed, she put on her cutest nightgown—a black one her aunt had brought back from Paris. It was silk and trimmed with lace. Her aunt was her father's sister and something of a "bad influence" (again, her mom's words). Hannah had made a decision.

When he appeared at three in the morning, she was waiting for him, sitting in the armchair next to her bed. She told him she had changed her mind.

"Are you sure?" he asked. "I don't want you to do something you don't want to do. I'm not that kind of vampire."

"Yes. But do it quickly before I chicken out," she ordered.

"You don't have to help me," he said.

"I know." She swallowed. "But I want to."

"I won't hurt you," he said.

She put a hand to her neck as if to protect it. "Promise?" How could she trust this strange boy? How could she risk her life to save him? But there was something about him—his sleepy dark eyes, his haunted expression—that drew her to him. Hannah was the type of girl who took in stray dogs and fixed birds' broken wings. Plus, there was that thing out there in the dark. She had to help him get away from it.

"Do it," she decided.

"Are you sure?"

She nodded briskly, as if she were at the doctor's office and had been asked to give consent to a particularly troublesome, but much-needed operation. She took off her glasses, pulled the right strap of her nightgown to the side, and arched her neck. She closed her eyes and prepared herself for the worst.

He walked over to her. He was so tall, and when he rested his hands on her bare skin, they were surprisingly warm to the touch. He pulled her closer to him and bent down.

"Wait," he said. "Open your eyes. Look at me."

She did. She stared at into his dark eyes, wondering what he was doing.

"They're beautiful—your eyes, I mean. You're

beautiful," he said. "I thought you should know."

She sighed and closed her eyes as his hand stroked her cheek.

"Thank you," he whispered.

She could feel his hot breath on her cheek, and then his lips brushed hers for a moment. He kissed her, pressing his lips firmly upon hers. She closed her eyes and kissed him back. His lips were so hot and wet.

Her first kiss, and from a vampire.

She felt his lips start to kiss the side of her mouth, and then the bottom of her chin, and then the base of her neck. This was it. She steeled herself for pain.

But he was right: there was very little. Just two tiny pinpricks, then a deep feeling of sleep. She could hear him sucking and swallowing, feel herself begin to get dizzy, woozy. Just like giving blood at the donor drive. Except she probably wouldn't get a doughnut after this.

She slumped in his arms, and he caught her. She could feel him walk her to the bed and lay her down on top of the sheets, then cover her with the duvet.

"Will I ever see you again?" she asked. It was hard to keep her eyes open. She was so tired. But she could see him vividly now. He seemed to glow. He looked more substantial.

"Maybe," he whispered. "But you'd be safer if you didn't."

She nodded dreamily, sinking into the pillows.

In the morning, she felt spent and logy, and told her mother she thought she was coming down with the flu and didn't feel like going to school. When she looked in the mirror, she saw nothing on her neck—there was no wound, no scar. Had nothing happened last night? Was she indeed going crazy? She felt around her skin with her fingertips and finally found it—a hardening of the skin, just two little bumps. Almost imperceptible, but there.

She'd made him tell her his name before she had agreed to help him.

Dylan, he'd said. *My name is Dylan Ward.*

Later that day, she dusted the plaque near the fireplace and looked at it closely. It was inscribed with a family crest, and underneath it read "Ward House." Wards were foster children. This had been a home for the lost. A safe house on Shelter Island.

Hannah thought of the beast out there in the night, rattling the windows, and hoped Dylan had made it to wherever he was going.

VENATOR RECORDS:
MARTIN

KINGSLEY MARTIN

Araquiel, Angel of Vengeance, the Angel with Two Faces
Birth Name: Kingsley Anderson Martin
Origin: Silver Blood Enmortal
Known Past Lives: Tiberius Gemellus (Rome)
Bondmate: None
Assigned Human Conduit: None
List of Human Familiars: None
Physical Characteristics:
    Hair: Dark brown
    Eyes: Blue
    Height: 6'1"

One of the Conclave's most trusted and skillful Venators, Kingsley Martin has a complicated past. He is a reformed Silver Blood—one who has been Corrupted by the Dark but continues to serve the Light. He was turned Croatan by Lucifer himself during Lucifer's reign as Caligula in ancient Rome. Kingsley was Tiberius Gemellus, the true heir of Caesar Tiberius, but Caligula, his adopted cousin, was favored and became emperor. Still, Gemellus loved Caligula like a brother, and the emperor returned his love by dooming him to eternal damnation.

Gemellus came back into the Blue Blood fold,

repenting his actions and learning to control the Abomination inside of him.

He was forgiven by Michael, and it is the Repository's belief that he was made the guardian of the Gate of Time. He has been a Venator at the service of the Regis ever since.

Throughout history, Kingsley has given much in service to the Coven. He is a key to understanding the Silver Blood methodology and physiology. (See Silver Bloods, in Appendix C, for more information.)

Assigned to investigate the murder of Aggie Carondolet, Kingsley enrolled as a student at Duchesne. With his cocky confidence, smoldering air of mystery, and devastating good looks {NOTE FROM RENFIELD: SCRIBES, ARE YOU SURE VENATOR MARTIN HASN'T HACKED INTO THIS FILE?}, Kingsley was a legend only a week after arriving at Duchesne. {NOTE TO RENFIELD FROM K.M. HI, RENNY!}

During the initial investigation he raised the first alarm that the Llewellyn family was not all it seemed, but the report was suppressed by Senator Llewellyn in the security committee and has only recently been declassified by Warden Barlow.

As noted in records, he set up Mimi to call up the

Silver Blood, but following the orders of the Regis (Charles Force) did it himself when she could not, proving without a doubt that the Croatan had found a way back into the world.

His latest assignment was to search for Jordan Llewellyn in Rio, and Mimi Force was assigned to his Venator team along with Sam and Ted Lennox. A dalliance between the Venator and {REDACTED/ RENFIELD: WAS THERE SOMETHING HERE? THIS FILE IS INCOMPLETE}. The team was successful in recovering the physical remains of the Watcher, and from his reports, we can safely assume that the Pistis Sophia is still alive.

Venator Martin was sent to Paris to hunt Leviathan but was instead spotted at the Force bonding at the Cathedral of St. John the Divine, in New York City. During the Silver Blood ambush he disappeared into the glom. He never returned, and the church showed traces of the *subvertio* spell. All traces of the Gate of Time and the path have been obliterated, and Venator Martin has not been seen since.

Current Status: Missing after Silver Blood attack. Believed to be trapped in the underworld.

Author's Note: This is a companion story to The Van Alen Legacy. *It is the continuation of the conversation between Mimi and Kingsley in chapter 47.*

THE VENATOR'S TALE
Kingsley's Story

*K*ingsley Martin took a long, slow sip from his glass of whiskey. Firewater, indeed. Not even close. But it would suffice for now. The waitress had mistaken his raised hand as a sign for another round. A mistake he didn't bother to correct since it appeared they would not be vacating their table anytime soon.

"Tell me everything," Mimi said, with a hint of desperation this time.

It was a while before he spoke, and when he did he directed his words toward the top of her head rather than looking her in the eyes. It was a trick he'd adopted in order to refrain from appearing nervous or insecure in her presence, making it seem as if he were distant and disinterested, when neither was the case. It was imperative that Mimi continue to have no idea how much she affected him.

"You want to know why Charles asked me to call the Silver Blood," he said finally.

"I assume it wasn't because he wanted to order a pizza," she cracked.

He let a smile play on his lips. Her brashness amused him. Azrael had always been blunt almost to the point of being rude, but there was a forthrightness to her that came through in every incarnation of her spirit. There was never a middle ground with her—she either loved you or loathed you; she was your best friend or your worst enemy.

"Oh forget it, you're not going to tell me anything," Mimi said. She stood up from the table and began to put on her coat, glaring down at him.

Always a game with this one, Kingsley thought. But he decided to call her bluff. She wanted to know, so why not tell her? She deserved to know. They all did. Not just Mimi but the entire Coven. She would hate him for what he did, or else find him pathetic and weak. But he was tired of keeping secrets. What was the point anymore, when everything was falling apart.

Kingsley put a hand on her wrist. "Sit down. I'll tell you everything you want to know," he said quietly.

Mimi slunk back down on to the banquette, looking like a spoiled child. "Begin at the beginning, when you first came to Duchesne. When you set me up."

He shook his head. "Understand, you were just another suspect who happened to be at the club the night Aggie Carondolet died. No one special. You were given the same treatment as the others. A Silver Blood sympathizer would be amenable to learning more about the Dark Matter. You were the only one who took the bait. I tried with Schuyler, but never got anywhere with her. Then with Bliss." He remembered what he had said to the Southern girl: "I am the same as you." If Bliss had been Croatan, she would have recognized the hidden meaning behind his words, that he was revealing his true nature, Silver Blood to Silver Blood. But Bliss had not responded to his confession.

"But you, my dear . . . you were a different story. You were very receptive to learning the dark magic. I had to hide it from your father. Charles would have protected you if he had known. Would have told me I was jumping to conclusions again." Kingsley looked apologetic. "Old allegiances and all . . ."

"You don't have to remind me," Mimi said, her face turning red. "I know what they say about Jack and me. That one day we'll be Benedict Arnold vampires."

He nodded. She knew as well as he did that Azrael and Abbadon would forever carry the stain of once being Lucifer's proudest generals.

"The *Incantation Demonata*," Mimi said. "Why did you do it?"

"I was ordered to by the Regis himself. It was a test, he said." Kingsley gripped his drink so tightly his knuckles turned white. "I thought he was playing me. Testing *my* loyalty maybe. But whatever. We just take orders, Venators. That's the way it is. If he wanted me to call up the Silver Blood, I was going to call up the Silver Blood."

"But why would Charles have you do such a thing. . . ." Mimi asked, horrified.

Kingsley gripped her arm across the small table. "Do you remember anything about Rome?"

"Some of it," she said. "It comes in bits and pieces—flashes—images—I remember the crisis, demons walking in daylight, hunting them down . . . and that last night in Lutetia . . ." She closed her eyes. "I remember telling Valerius that Sophia was wrong—there was no way Caligula had turned—that Cassius was just jealous as usual—but then . . . we saw it."

Kingsley nodded. Caligula and his crimson eyes with the silver pupils. The unmistakable sign of Corruption. Agrippina Azrael and Valerius Abbadon had led the emperor down to the path, down to the newly forged gate, where Cassius—Michael—was waiting. The battle had not been easily won. But they had done it. Sent the Devil down to Hell.

"But what does Rome have to do with what happened in the Repository?" Mimi asked.

"Well, for starters, since the incantation worked, it proved that Silver Bloods still existed, and that they had a way into our world. Because Charles didn't believe it—not at first, not even with all the killings. I don't think he truly accepts it now. And he wanted to keep it from the Committee. But he had to do something if he was wrong—so he sent me to Corcovado. Because if they were back, that's the first place they would go—to free Leviathan."

Mimi nodded, taking it all in.

"Do you know anything about the gates? About the Order of the Seven?" Kingsley asked.

Mimi shrugged. "I don't think I was privy to that

meeting. I was surprised as anyone to find that Michael had chosen to father us for this cycle. He knows we weren't huge fans of the so-called Uncorrupted. At least, I never was."

Kingsley filled her in on what he knew about the Gates of Hell and the guardians ordered to protect them, as well as his part in it. "The gates keep the paths secure and the demons in the underworld. The gates should have stopped the incantation from working. But they didn't. That was the test. The Silver Blood was able to break through the barrier. Charles suspects that Lucifer has been able to find a way into our world that we did not expect, did not foresee."

"But how?"

"How indeed . . . especially since the Conclave took care of the biggest threat."

"Oh god. I had totally forgotten about that." Mimi said, her palms at her cheeks, as if to hide from the truth. "It was you, wasn't it? You were the one who took Gabrielle after I wasn't brave enough to do it myself."

Kingsley nodded. The twins had been given the task, but had balked at the very *wrongness* of it—and so he and Forsyth had kidnapped Gabrielle from her room. He remembered everything. The silent birth, the frightened midwives, then Charles and Lawrence taking the baby . . . the burned swaddling clothes, the ghastly smell of death all around. Then Gabrielle waking up with no memory of her ordeal or even that she'd borne a child.

"I don't think any of us have ever forgiven ourselves for what we did that night. Not me, not Lawrence, not Charles, not Forsyth. War is a terrible thing. There is no room for mercy." Kingsley's face was drawn, hollow. He didn't feel much like talking anymore. Poor Lawrence, his friend and mentor. And now Charles, lost as well. "Well. That's everything."

"Oh, Kingsley," Mimi said gently.

Kingsley looked up, surprised to find Mimi with tears in her eyes. She put a soft hand to his cheek.

She looked at him in silence, and in her eyes he found forgiveness and understanding, the two things he hoped for the most and expected the least. In Rio, Kingsley felt he had taken advantage of the situation a little bit— they had been so tired after their trek through he jungle, she couldn't have been in her right mind when she'd knocked on his door that night, when she had sought comfort in his kisses. That was why he had kept her at arm's length ever since.

But she was here now. And she was the one leaning toward him. "I'm so sorry. I'm so sorry, baby," Mimi was saying.

They were words he had waited a lifetime—many lifetimes—to hear, and that they came from Azrael, she who had spurned him for centuries (Abbadon wasn't the only one who had pined for one he could not have). She had mocked him in Rome—haughty, beautiful Agrippina, who had no time for Gemellus, no time at all for a weakling such as himself—a rare, solitary soul, never bound. Gemellus, who had loved and worshipped her from afar, she who was in his arms now. . . .

Victory was sweet. Who knew that the path to a woman's heart was through the soul of an honest man?

Kingsley Martin would never understand women. But that was all right. He didn't need to understand Mimi. All he had to do was love her, and he could do that.

THE VAN ALEN LEGACY
AND THE PATHS OF THE DEAD

With his dying breath, Lawrence Van Alen revealed a secret to Schuyler: she was the heir not just of the Van Alen name but to a very important legacy. He instructed her to find out more from Charles, but during the Silver Blood ambush at the *Bal des Vampires* in Paris, Charles became trapped in the *subvertio*, the White Darkness, and was unable to disclose what he knew.

However, when Schuyler returned to New York, Allegra woke up from her coma, stirred from her unconscious state by a deep memory of another daughter, and within the safety of the glom, she was able to tell Schuyler the history of the Gates of Hell and the Paths of the Dead.

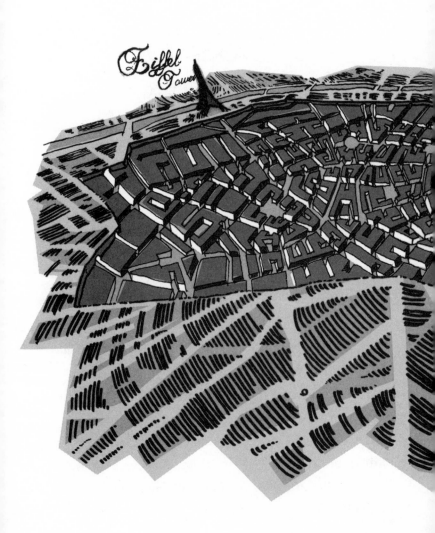
Eiffel Tower

In the days before the battle in Heaven and Lucifer's fall, the paths between the worlds were open. Angels moved freely between Heaven, Earth, and the underworld. After the Fall, when Lucifer and his army of angels were cast out, the way to Paradise was shut forever. But the seven paths to the underworld remained open. These were the Paths of the Dead.

In Rome, before Caligula was revealed as the Dark Prince, Michael, as Cassius, served as the emperor's closest adviser. When Caligula found that one of the Paths of the Dead was anchored below the city of Lutetia, Cassius convinced him to let him forge a gate there to keep the demons at bay. Caligula stole the key from Cassius and, revealing his true nature as Lucifer, unleashed Abomination upon the world. The battle of Rome ensued. At the end, Agrippina and Valerius (Azrael and Abbadon) were able to coax Caligula to the newly forged gate, where Cassius (Michael) sent him to Hell, locking the gate behind him.

After Rome, Michael ordered the Blue Bloods to locate the six other paths and build gates upon them to secure the divisions between the worlds and keep Earth safe from the creatures of the underworld. The guardians, keepers of the Gates of Hell, were known as the Order of the Seven, one from each of the seven original families of the Conclave. The guardians scattered across the earth, unknown to one another but passing down their knowledge through the generations.

The guardians were to keep the gates secure, and the gates, imbued with the celestial power of the angels, were supposed to keep the world safe from the Prince of Darkness and the legions at his command. But with the growing number of Silver Blood attacks over the centuries, Lawrence suspected that somehow, the gates were failing and that Lucifer was plotting a way back from the underworld.

Schuyler must now continue Lawrence's search for the gates and their guardians before the Silver Bloods are able to destroy them all and bring about a second Great War. This is the Van Alen Legacy. Charles resented the Van Alen Legacy, displeased that Lawrence harbored deep doubts concerning the strength of the gates he forged centuries ago. The Gates of Hell must hold, or all the world will fall with their destruction.

THE GATES OF HELL

*T*he Gates of Hell are located around the world, placed upon the seven paths to the underworld. The following are the three known gates so far:

The Gate of Vengeance was Leviathan's prison on Corcovado. Lawrence Van Alen was its gatekeeper. With his murder of an innocent (Dylan, in the guise of Lucifer), the gate was opened, but it was a *solom bicallis*, which can only be used once. Once Leviathan came through it, the path was closed to all.

The Gate of Time was created during the reign of Caligula, who had discovered a path underneath the underground city of Lutetia (now located in present-day Paris). Lucifer and Leviathan assumed that Michael was its guardian. The Silver Bloods planned to open the gate by destroying its keeper. But when they released the *subvertio*, all they found was an intersection, which created a time vacuum. The true keeper of the Gate of Time is Kingsley Martin, who had moved the gate underneath the Cathedral of St. John the Divine in New York City; an unfinished church, which meant it was not fully consecrated, and was a place of worship that a Silver Blood like Kingsley could enter.

The third gate is known as **The Gate of Promise**. Lawrence, who left more than fifty-five notebooks with his Conduit, Anderson, believed its guardians are still in Florence.

There are no other gates known to the Repository at this time.

REVKJAVIK*

OSLO*

PARIS

BARCELO

NY

RIO

* POSSIBLE GATE

SCHUYLER'S WORL

MAP OF THE GATES

THE FALLEN BRETHREN: HOUSE OF THE MORNINGSTAR

The Morningstar, Lightbringer, Prince of Heaven,
Prince of Darkness, Archangel of the Dawn
Known Past Lives: Gaius Caligula (Rome)

Phosphorus Lucifer, leader of the Fallen, king of the Silver Bloods, was the Crown Prince of Heaven, the most beautiful and powerful of all the angels until he chose to challenge the Almighty in the War for the Heavenly Kingdom. Upon his defeat, he awoke on Earth to find himself a vampyre, among the cursed and expelled from Paradise. He refused to make peace with Michael and Gabrielle, the angels who vanquished him, or with Abbadon and Azrael, his greatest friends, who betrayed him at the last. Not much is known about the Dark Prince ever since he and his loyal followers severed their ties to the Coven sometime during the reign of Menes, in the kingdom of Egypt, when they rose up in rebellion. His last known interaction with the Blue Blood community came in the battle of Rome, when he was revealed as the mad emperor Caligula.

It is said that in his true form, his presence is so bright it hurts to look directly at him. As Caligula, he

was able to hide his true identity until Julia Livilla, the Pistis Sophia, discovered the truth. As Lucifer has been banished to the underworld since his defeat at the battle of Rome, the Repository is still unclear as to how, when, and where in history he fathered a child with Allegra.
{INFORMATION REDACTED BY ORDER OF REGIS}

Recovered from Bliss Llewellyn's journal (unverified) is a decription of a man she called "the Visitor," who appears as a handsome gentleman in a white suit with molten gold hair and clear blue eyes, whose beauty is remote and chilling, a description often attributed to the image of Lucifer by those who claim to have seen him in their dreams.

Venator reports from the attack at St. John the Divine indicate that the Dark Prince battled Abbadon and Azrael in the glom, but was unable to escape the underworld, as Venator Martin released the *subvertio* and obliterated the path back to the living world.

Current Status: Unknown. Presumed trapped in the underworld.

LEVIATHAN TRAPPED UNDERNEATH THE GATE OF VENGEANCE

LEVIATHAN

The Giant, the Kraken, Goliath of the Glom
Known Past Lives: Marcus Agrippa (Rome)

Vesperus Leviathan, brother to the Dark Prince, was known as one of the cruelest Silver Bloods who ever walked the earth. He is partial to wearing dark cloaks and a hood that covers his face, described by those who have had the misfortune to see it as red and black, twisted, scarred, and burned from Hell's flames.

He was captured in {DATE REDACTED} by Gabrielle and imprisoned into the rock under Corcovado, the only place on Earth that could contain his power. Metraton (Lawrence Van Alen) was his gatekeeper and jailer, and Corcovado was put under twenty-four hour surveillance by the Venator elite.

A crafty plan hatched by the traitor Silver Bloods of the Conclave, Nan Cutler and Forsyth Llewellyn, led Metraton to unknowingly destroy Leviathan's prison bonds when he slaughtered an innocent (Dylan Ward, whose image had been manipulated to look like Lucifer's). Reports from the European Coven indicate that Leviathan was in attendance at the *Bal des Vampires*, and those who survived the attack at St. John's Cathedral testified that they witnessed Leviathan abduct Schuyler Van Alen before disappearing into the glom. Since Venator Martin released the *subvertio*, however, it is safe to assume that with the destruction of the path to the underworld, Leviathan is safely in Hell once again.

```
Current Status: Missing. Believed to be
trapped in the underworld.
```

NAN CUTLER

Harbonah, Angel of Annihilation
Origin: February 12, 1917, New York, New York
Known Past Lives: Anna Stamersly (Newport),
Aemilia Lepida (Rome)

The second-highest-ranking Blue Blood in the Coven, Nan Cutler served as Regent on the Conclave. She was notable for her loyalty, ferocity, and in this cycle, for a striking raven stripe through her white hair. As Aemilia Lepida, a trusted friend to Cassius (Michael) and Junia Tertia (Allegra), she was on the front lines in the battle in Rome.

Warden Cutler was entrusted with the task of investigating young vampires for the mark of Silver Blood Corruption after the attack on the Repository. She affixed the false mark of Lucifer upon Mimi Force and cleared Bliss Llewellyn from suspicion. The Repository believes that Nan Cutler was the mastermind behind the slaughter of the Conclave in Rio.

According to the Venator report, Mimi Force believed she had killed Warden Cutler in the battle. However, during their search for Jordan Llewellyn, the Venators came upon the Warden, who had survived the Black Fire and was now a living corpse. The Venators believe Warden Cutler had kidnapped Jordan Llewellyn on that fateful night and then posed as her grandmother, torturing her for information on the Order of the Seven, until she killed the girl (but not the spirit of the Watcher). According to Venator Martin, it is safe to assume that Warden Cutler is no longer with us.

```
Current Status: Finished. Slain by
Venator Martin.
```

THE SEVEN RULING HOUSES
OF THE CONCLAVE

lue Blood society is hierarchical and orga-
nized. The Conclave is the highest ruling
body of the Coven. There are seven main houses that
serve on the council as an homage to the seven original ruling families who founded it. Conclave members
may also include Elders and Wardens who are not affiliated with any particular house but who have been
nominated to serve by its current membership. However, the Code of the Vampires mandates that a representative from each of the seven houses is needed for
a quorum of seven to pass changes to the Code of the
Vampires and to call for a White Vote, the election of
a new Regis.

Domus Magnificat: House of Riches Traditionally the seat of the wealthiest family in the Coven, the
House of Riches is currently represented by Josiah
Rockefeller Archibald, whose family built Rockefeller
Center. The House of Riches is responsible for the
health of the Coven's financial security. Other families
who have held this position include the Schlumbergers
and the Whitneys.

**Domus Stella Aquillo: House of the Northern
Star** The House of the Northern Star spearheads one
of the biggest benefactors of art programs in the country, and is currently represented by Ambrose Barlow.

Domus Veritas: House of the Venators Represented by Abe Tompkins, the House of the Venators is
the voice of the Truth Seekers on the council and responsible for the security and protection of the Coven.
Other families who have held this position include the
Van Horns.

Domus Preposito: House of the Stewards The
seat on the council traditionally awarded to the family of the Regent, the House of the Stewards was

represented by Forsyth Llewellyn until his disgrace and disappearance, and before him by Nan Cutler. Other families who have held this position include the Stewart family, who derived their last name from having held this post for many centuries.

Domus Domina: House of the Gray Lady, also known more commonly as the House of Records The position in the council that oversees the records of the cycles of Expression, Expulsion, and Evolution. Currently represented by Minerva Morgan, this seat was formerly filled by the Carondolet family.

Domus Lamia: House of the Vampyres The House of the Vampyres oversees vampire–human relations, and its representative is also the head of the Conspiracy Subcommittee, which keeps the false myths and misleading legends about the Blue Bloods alive in Red Blood society. Currently represented by Seymour Corrigan, who is cousin to Edmund Oelrich, the Chief Warden who perished in the Rio massacre.

Domus Fortis Valerius Incorruptus: House of the Pure Blood, of the Uncorrupted, of the

Valiant and the Strong, Protector of the Garden, Commander of the Lord's Armies The seat on the council given to the family of the reigning Regis, since the beginning of time the seat has been held by Michael and Gabrielle's line; the Van Alen line is currently represented by Mimi Force since Charles Force's disappearance.

THE COMMITTEE

"The Committee" is Blue Blood shorthand for the vast number of charitable causes, educational institutions, and foundations that are run by the Coven membership. The Committee has been responsible for the preservation of some of New York's most important landmarks and has funded many of the city's most prestigious cultural institutions. Under its official public name, the New York Blood Bank, it has raised money for blood research, HIV and AIDS, and hemophilia. To outsiders, it appears snobby, cliquish, and exclusive to the extreme; to insiders, it is sovereign.

Committee members are called Wardens. All Blue Blood families registered with the Coven are invited to join; most individuals receive their membership invitation around the age of fifteen, coinciding with their Transformation into immortal. Under his tenure as Regis, Lawrence Van Alen opened the Committee membership to include human Conduits; this policy was quickly revoked by Forsyth Llewellyn. It has yet to be reinstated.

The Committee's Chief Warden is in charge of educating and ushering the newest generation of vampires to adulthood and imbuing them with the spirit of the vampires' mission on Earth: to bring light, truth, beauty, and art, and to bring Paradise to their Earthly home.

APPENDIX A:

List of Secondary Characters

Abeville, Toby: Blue Blood groom who gets bonded in Bali to Daisy Van Horn.

Adriana: Housekeeper at the Duchesne school

Almeida, Don Alfonso ("Alfie"): An Elder from the South American Coven, his family is part of the Blue Blood contingent that moved to Brazil in 1808, when the Portuguese royal family and many nobles chose to flee from, rather than fight, the Red Blood conqueror Napoleon. The Rio Conclave said he went missing during his yearly sojourn into the Andes, and it was suspected that he had fallen victim to a Silver Blood attack. He returned seemingly unharmed, but we now believe he had been Corrupted in a Silver Blood ruse to bring the New York Conclave to Rio for slaughter. He hosted the dinner party where they were all murdered.

Almeida, Doña Beatrice: The wife of Alfonso Almeida, suspected to have also been Corrupted by the Silver Bloods

Amory, Summer: A Blue Blood debutante found drained by a Silver Blood in her penthouse apartment in Trump Tower. Her last name is frequently misspelled as "Armory" in the Repository Files (interns: please correct immediately).

Anders, George: One of the former Conduits who now serves as a librarian at the Repository

Anderson, Christopher: Lawrence Van Alen's human Conduit for almost seventy years. After Lawrence's murder on Corcovado, Anderson chose freedom and forced amnesia rather than a position as a Repository scribe, but not before sending Schuyler and Oliver to Countess Isabelle for help.

Andrews, James, M.D.: Dr. Andrews was the doctor in charge of Dylan Ward at Transitions rehabilitation center.

Anka (No Last Name Given): The designer of Stitched for Civilization, a high-end jeans line. She hired Schuyler and Bliss for an advertising campaign.

Archibald, Josiah Rockefeller: Retired from the Conclave for years, he was called back to serve as Inquisitor after the Rio Massacre. As one of the seven ruling Wardens, he represents Domus Magnificat, the House of Riches.

Bank, Charlie: Another teenage vampire sent to Transitions for "rehab" during his Transformation

Barlow, Ambrose: One of the oldest living Elders in this cycle, Ambrose Barlow was relieved from emeritus status and called back to duty in the Conclave after the Rio Massacre. In Rome he was Caligula's foreman Brittanicus before Caligula's Corruption was discovered. In *The Van Alen Legacy* (Repository Record #404), when Bliss Llewellyn heard Forsyth and the Visitor mocking him, she assumed he must be one of the good guys and sent him an anonymous letter warning him that Forsyth was dangerous. Though Ambrose shared this letter with Minerva Morgan and Mimi, he was not strong enough to vote against Forsyth in the White Vote. He represents Domus Stella Aquillo, House of the Northern Star.

Barlow, Margery: Elder emeritus, wife of Ambrose

Campbell, Superintendent: Police official assigned to investigate the disappearance of Maggie Stanford

Carondolet, Augusta ("Aggie"): A Blue Blood student at Duchesne and one of Mimi's crew of clones (platinum hair, spoiled-brattitude), Aggie was the first victim of the New York slayings. The Red Bloods were told her death was caused by a drug overdose, but in reality she was found fully drained in a back room at Block 122.

Carondolet, Cushing and Sloane: Aggie's parents; they were kicked out of the Conclave for a time following her death for showing anti-Committee sentiment and calling for the White Vote. They returned to serve on the council after

Lawrence Van Alen was made Regis. The couple perished during the Rio massacre.

Carter, Muriel ("Muffie") Astor: One of most popular Blue Blood socialites, she was educated at Miss Porter's and Vassar and enjoyed a successful career in public relations before marrying Dr. Sheldon Carter. She is the hostess of an annual fashion show at her Hamptons estate, benefiting the New York Blood Bank, where Bliss made her return to modeling after the tragedy in Rio.

Carter, Sheldon, M.D.: A Blue Blood plastic surgeon and Muffie Astor's husband

Castañeda, Don Alejandro: Blue Blood heir to his father's sugar and beverage fortune, whose bonding to Danielle Russell was planned by Lizbet Tilton

Chantal: The booking editor of *Chic* magazine; a small, short, pinched-looking woman with a pixie haircut and cat's-eye glasses

Chen, Dehua: A young vampire from the Blue Blood coven based in Shanghai. Xi Wangmu, Angel of Immortality, was presented at the Four Hundred Ball along with her twin, Deming Chen.

Chen, Deming: A young vampire from the Blue Blood Coven based in Shanghai. Kuan Yin, Angel of Mercy, was presented at the Four Hundred Ball in New York. Twin to Dehua Chen.

Corrigan, Seymour: A Warden emeritus called back to duty in the Conclave after Rio. He led the proceedings at the White Vote called by Forsyth Llewellyn.

Coubertin, Baron de: The baron served as human Conduit to the Countess of Paris and was the key to an audience with her. The demon Leviathan shape-shifted into his form at the *Bal des Vampires*, and the real Baron de Coubertin was found dead in the River Seine the next day.

Cushing, John, Reverend: Officiated at the wedding of Caroline Vanderbilt to Alfred, Lord Burlington

Cyrus: Rolf Morgan's "spastic showrunner" who runs and produces Rolf's fashion shows

Danilo: Mimi's hairdresser

Devonshire, Duke and Duchess of: The parents of Alfred, Lord Burlington

Doris: Forsyth Llewellyn's secretary

Duchesne, Margeurite: Belgian governess to the Flood heiresses who founded the Duchesne School

Dupont, Eliza: Priscilla's niece who took her place on the Conclave after Priscilla's untimely demise

Dupont, Gina: Charles Force's human familiar, whom Mimi understands is more than her father's mistress. Gina is unrelated to the Blue Blood Duponts.

Dupont, Priscilla: Chief Warden and head of the Committee, she was a well-known Blue Blood socialite whose regal visage regularly graced the weekly social columns. Her untimely death during the attack at the Repository ushered in the rule of Lawrence Van Alen, as the Coven could no longer deny the return of the Silver Bloods.

Essex, Marquis of: Best man at the wedding of Lord Burlington and Caroline Vanderbilt, following the disappearance of Lord Burlington's former fiancée, Maggie Stanford

Farnsworth, Linda: A short, squat woman with crinkly hair and an overall dowdy appearance, which is surprising considering her position as founder of Farnsworth Models. Linda's girls, including Bliss, Mimi, and Schuyler, grace the runways of Bryant Park, the billboards of Times Square, and the pages of *Chic* magazine.

Flood, Armstrong, Captain: Founder of the Flood Oil Company

Flood, Rose Elizabeth: Wife of Captain Armstrong Flood who donated the family home (Flood mansion) to the Duchesne School when her three daughters died during the sinking of the S.S. *Endeavor* during an Atlantic crossing.

Frost, Brannon: The Blue Blood editor in chief of *Chic* magazine

Getty, Natalie: A Blue Blood teen killed by Silver Bloods in the New York slayings

Hazard, Patricia, M.D.: Oliver's aunt and the Blue Bloods' trusted doctor, she watches over the New York Coven's health at her posh Fifth Avenue office. In particular, she observes their Transformations, especially Schuyler's unusual case as half vampire, half human.

Henri of Orleans, Crown Prince of France (deposed), also known as Henri Bourbon and Henri, Count of Paris: The late Blue Blood husband of Countess Isabelle, he would have been heir to the French throne had the Revolution never happened. Isabelle took his position as Regis of the European Conclave after his passing from the current cycle.

Isabelle of Orleans, the Countess of Paris: Hostess of the *Bal des Vampires* and former owner of the Hôtel Lambert, the countess is the Regis of the European Conclave and former friend of Lawrence and Cordelia Van Alen. Schuyler and Oliver traveled to Paris seek her aid when the New York Conclave decided that Schuyler was responsible for Lawrence's death. The American and the European covens became estranged when the Blue Bloods left the Old World. Isabelle never had much faith in Michael as Regis. She is an imposing woman, regal and beautiful, with coal-black hair. At the end of *The Van Alen Legacy*, Schuyler, now with Jack, finally was granted an audience with the countess, who gave them refuge and protection. However, in a twist, it was revealed that the countess was Drusilla in a past cycle, Caligula's beloved sister, and perhaps her old allegiance to Lucifer still runs deep.

Jackson, Hattie: Cordelia and Schuyler Van Alen's loyal maid, she and Julius watch over the house on Riverside Drive and essentially raised the (for all intents and purposes) motherless Schuyler.

Jackson, Julius: Cordelia Van Alen's personal driver. Married to Hattie.

Jones, Jonas: The famously incorrigible Blue Blood fashion photographer and Duchesne alum; also a filmmaker and painter

Keaton, Alice: Chantal's assistant at *Chic*, who goes by her last name

Lennox, Sam and Ted: Twin brothers and Venators on Mimi and Kingsley's team

Leslie, Honor: Another teenage vampire sent to Transitions for "rehab" during her transformation

Llewellyn, Dennis (Pap-Pap): Bliss's beloved grandfather and Forsyth's father, he was a rebel from a Texas oil family who stayed East after boarding school, married a Connecticut debutante, and raised his family on Fifth Avenue until the stock market sent them back to the Texas homestead.

Manuela: The Llewellyn family's maid who works in their Hamptons property

Marie: Lawrence Van Alen's Italian landlady whom he impersonates when Schuyler chases him through the canals of Venice

McCall, Wesley: Another vampire teen at Transitions. He told Ally Elli about Dylan's memorial service, who in turn told Bliss.

Morgan, Minerva: Along with Ambrose Barlow, one of the oldest living Elders, Minerva Morgan was called back to duty in the Conclave. She was one of Cordelia Van Alen's oldest friends and former chairwoman of the New York Garden Society. Like Ambrose, she was suspicious of Forsyth but too weak to vote against him in the White Vote.

Morgan, Randy: Rolf's wife and first model, the quintessential "Morgan" girl

Morgan, Rolf: A designer of preppie, old-boy style. He selected Bliss as the new face of his line.

Oelrich, Edmund: A famous art historian and gallery owner in his private life, in the Blue Blood realm he replaced Priscilla Dupont as Chief Warden after she was killed by a Silver Blood. Perished in the Rio massacre.

Phillips, Henri: Bliss's modeling agent, who visits her to lend his condolences and to offer her a job

Potter, Charlotte: The woman Bliss was told was the mother she never knew. She was supposedly a schoolteacher her father met on his first campaign trail, but there are no wedding albums or heirlooms. It is the Repository's belief that Charlotte Potter is a fictional creation, a lie told by Forsyth Llewellyn.

Renfield: One of the older and more crotchety human librarians at the Repository. He takes his job very seriously.

Riberio, Yana: A young vampire of the Rio Coven. She was feared missing but had only absconded with her boyfriend. This may have been a Silver Blood ruse to bring about the Rio massacre.

Rockefeller, Dorothea: Conclave Elder who perished during the Rio massacre. She also guest-lectured at a Committee meeting and taught the fledgling vampires how to transform themselves into smoke, fog, or air (the *mutatio*).

Russell, Danielle: Another of Lizbet Tilton's Blue Blood clients. A recent Brown grad bonded to her twin, Don Alejandro Castañeda.

Schlessinger, Landon: A Blue Blood teen killed during the New York slayings

Schlumberger, Esme: Conclave Elder who perished during the Rio massacre. She called Alfonso Almeida an "old coot" during a Conclave meeting.

Shriver, Morgan: The cute nineteen-year-old college student who became Bliss's first human familiar on a photo shoot in Montserrat. Bliss came close to draining him accidentally, but he recovered, only to become infatuated with her.

Smith, Perfection: The makeup artist on Bliss and Schuyler's Stitched for Civilization shoot

Sorboba, Sarina: Incredibly tall Eastern European model who was much favored by fashion designers

Stewart, Brooks: Conclave Elder who perished during the Rio massacre. Had a coughing fit when Kingsley Martin appears, alive and unharmed, during a Conclave meeting.

St. James, Grayson: A Blue Blood teen killed during the New York slayings

Sully: Mimi and Jack's chauffeur

Tilton, Elizabeth (Lizbet): The event planner Mimi hired to plan her bonding to Jack; famous for her lavish events

Tompkins, Abe: An Elder, once emeritus on the Conclave, called back to duty after the slaughter in Rio. As a former Venator he represents Domus Veritas, House of the Venators.

Vanderbilt, Ava: Younger sister of Caroline and maid of honor at her sister's wedding to Lord Burlington in 1872

Vanderbilt, Caroline: Eldest daughter of Admiral and Mrs. Vanderbilt who marries Lord Burlington after the disappearance of his fiancée, Maggie Stanford

Vanderbilt, Admiral Sloane and Elizabeth: Parents of the Vanderbilt girls, Ava and Caroline

Van Horn, Daisy: Blue Blood bride who has a destination bonding to Toby Abeville in Bali

Van Horn, Dashiell: Conclave Elder who persished during the Rio massacre. Daisy is his daughter.

Verdugo, Balthazar: The designer at Muffie Astor Carter's annual Hamptons fashion show

Whitney, Alice: Conclave Elder who represents the House of the Seven Sisters

Wilcox, Patrice: The stern, no-nonsense, all-black-wearing fashion director of *Chic*

Partial List of Duchesne Students

Blue Blood Students

Applegate, Cicely: Part of Mimi Force's crew of clones

Crandall, Piper: The school's biggest gossip and a valuable Repository intern

Cutting, Bryce: Good friend to Jack Force; member of the lacrosse team

Forbes, Lucy: Head Girl. Senior (Repository Record #303 misidentified as a Red Blood, possibly due to Venator Force's dislike of her). Reported that Mimi abused her human familiars by not waiting the mandatory forty-eight-hour rest period before feeding on them again.

Frost, Willow: Brannon Frost's daughter

Harris, Lissy: A friend of Mimi's and an attendant at her wedding in Newport during an earlier cycle

Kemble, Susan ("Soos")

Kernochan, Francis ("Froggy")

Kip, James Andrew (Jamie): Red Blood Allison Ellison's boyfriend; also dated Ava Breton, another Red Blood

King, Rufus

Langdon, Bozeman ("Booze")

McMillan, Blair: His father owns the largest record label in the world

Robinson, Bennet: Mimi supposedly threw up on his terrace during a DisOrientation party her freshman year

Sheridan, Katie: A friend of Mimi's

Tuckerman, Carter: Junior Committee secretary

Van Rensslaer, Stella

Red Blood Students

While the students at Duchesne mostly come from old Blue Blood families, a number of Red Bloods have also been allowed to enroll. Most of the human families are either very wealthy or connected to the Blue Bloods in some way. There are also students who have been granted financial aid and scholarships, in order to make the school more "diverse."

Breton, Ava: A very popular Red Blood in Bliss's class, whose friends are almost all Blue Bloods, though she doesn't know it. She was Jamie Kip's familiar and girlfriend before he ditched her for Allison Ellison.

Ellison, Allison (Ally Elli): A Red Blood from Duchesne and Jamie Kip's girlfriend and human familiar. A scholarship kid from Queens, she is nonetheless very popular for her outer-borough "exoticism." Ally told Bliss about Dylan's memorial service and the drug overdose cover-up of his death.

Mullins, Kitty: Jack's human familiar; however, it appears he did not make use of the relationship very much, as Mimi describes him as always "tired and drained."

Walsh, Haley: A girl in Bliss's Ancient Civilizations class who thinks "Senior year is going to rock!"

Partial List of Duchesne Faculty and Administration

Mr. Anthony: A boyish recent Yale grad and (overly) enthusiastic chemistry teacher. Dismissed from Duchesne for getting a student pregnant.

Mr. Korgan: Mr. Anthony's boring, old replacement

Cecil Malloy: Dean of Students at Duchesne. Not an alum but "a very adequate facsimile."

Mr. Orion: A mustachioed, curly-haired Brown graduate with a penchant for oversized sweaters. He teaches Ethics and English.

Madame Fraley: French teacher who looks like she's been at the school since the 1880s (most likely a Blue Blood Enmortal)

APPENDIX B:

A Partial List of Canine Familiars

Canine familiars are part of a vampire's soul transferred into the physical world to protect young Blue Bloods until they come into complete control of their powers. Canine protectors routinely merge back into the Blue Blood upon completion of their mission. The current generation of Blue Bloods is the most talented yet, and because none of the canine familiars have made an appearance since the attack at the cathedral, we may conclude that perhaps the young Blue Bloods are in close to full possession of their abilities. In the past, traumatic events have shown to make a young vampire grow up more quickly than expected.

BEAUTY

Schuyler Van Alen
Bloodhound (highest rank)

According to Schuyler's journal (left in the 101st Street mansion and discovered by the Repository upon her disappearance), Beauty followed her home one day.

MISS ELLIE

Bliss Llewellyn

Chihuahua

Bliss's Chihuahua canine familiar, named after her favorite character on *Dallas*

PATCH

Jack Force

Bloodhound (highest rank)

Jack's canine familiar, a bloodhound he found the same evening that Mimi found Pookie

POOKIE

Mimi Force

Chow chow

Mimi's canine familiar, a chow she found on the beach at the Hamptons

SNOW WHITE

Aggie Carondolet

Chihuahua

Aggie Carondolet's Chihuahua canine familiar, which she liked to dress in outfits that matched her own

APPENDIX C:
Dictionary of Terms

Author's Note: All words in italic are from the Sacred Language.

Abomination: Silver Bloods are called Abominations because they are vampires who have sucked the blood of their own kind and consumed their spirit. They carry the tortured souls of their victims in one body.

Absed Abysso: "Go back to Hell." A command to a banish a Silver Blood back to its rightful home

Adventurers Club: An elite Blue Blood organization founded in the early eighteenth century as a meeting place for like-minded globe-trotters eager to document and share their research and theories on natural and geographic phenomenon, located across from the Knickerbocker Club and Metropolitan Museum of Art on Fifth Avenue

Advoco Adiuvo: An invocation that Schuyler uses, per Cordelia's instructions, so Lawrence will recognize her in Venice

Alienari: A common trick of the Silver Bloods, used to disguise themselves as someone else

Altithronus: Audio recordings kept in the Repository of History

Animadverto: The vampire ability of "intelligent sight," or an immense and perfect photographic memory so powerful a vampire has the ability to read and remember entire libraries

Aperio Oris: An incantation demanding that one reveal oneself

Argento Croatus: Silver Blood

Bal des Vampires: A party and congress held every other year by the European Coven. It was to be the party to end all parties at the Hôtel Lambert before it was given over to its new owners. The celebration was infiltrated by Silver Bloods hunting for Schuyler.

Bivio: A crossroads; a primal source of strength and power

Black Fire: The only thing that can destroy the *sangre azul* and kill an immortal vampire

Black Spells: Spells pertaining to the Dark Matter

Blade of Justice: Michael's sword, one of only two archangels'

swords in the world, the other being Gabrielle's. Only an archangel's sword can kill another archangel.

Blood Bond: The holy matrimony and immortal bond between two vampires whose souls were twinned in Heaven. Occasionally vampire twins are born as siblings in the human world. Bondmates are obligated to renew their vows in every cycle with a ceremony, usually in their twenty-first year, when they have come into their memories and powers and can recognize their spouse in his or her new physical shell. All it takes is for the couple to exchange the vow "I give myself to you" to become irrevocably one for that cycle. Only one couple in Blue Blood history has broken this bond—when Gabrielle forsook Michael for her human familiar.

After the bond, the vampires are stronger, but if the bond is broken, the betrayed vampire may bring the other to a blood trial, to face a sentence of death.

Blood-lock: The most powerful security system in the Blue Blood arsenal; it only opens for the blood of an angel

Blood Manifest (Transformation): The process in which a vampire's blue blood cells, their vampire DNA, starts to take over, typically around age fifteen. The fangs grow in, the body switches from needing nourishment from food to needing nourishment from human blood, memories of previous cycles start to come back, and specific powers begin to manifest. The process can make the young vampire weak, and may include memory shock, dizziness, and sickness.

Blood Marks: The blue marks that appear on the arms of young vampires during their Transformation. They look like a sapphire light shining through the skin. The marks are a map of the vampire's personal histories—the *sangre azul* asserting itself.

Blood Trial: The process in which the most serious offenses against the Code of the Vampires are resolved. It requires the blood and memories of the accused to be consumed in order to tell true memory from false. The trial can only be performed by Gabrielle, as one of the highest-ranking Venators. Schuyler inherited her mother's gift. The Blood Trial involves a great risk of temptation for the one who performs it. If the accused is found guilty, the offender's blood will be burned in complete destruction.

Blue Bloods: Vampires: fallen angels doomed to live their eternal lives on Earth. They have superhuman speed, hyper-intelligence, a photographic memory, and heightened senses. They live by the Code of the Vampires, which is a pledge to bring peace and beauty to the world. They do not abuse their human familiars or feed on their own kind.

Book of Laws: The Blue Blood record of all investigations, judgments, and punishments

Breath of God: The ability of any Blue Blood to bring light to the tunnels of Lutetia with a wave of the hand above a torch

Burning: The burning the blood of a vampire, thus destroying the immortal blood and all its memories

The Call: The hypnotizing seduction a vampire can use to call a human to him or her for the *Caerimonia Osculor*

Caerimonia Osculor (**the Sacred Kiss**): The regulated ritual of feeding on a human familiar's blood. There are stringent rules, as no human is ever to be abused or fully drained. The Code of the Vampires forbids performing the kiss on another vampire. The Sacred Kiss marks a human as the vampire's own—they will always be bonded.

Candidus Suffragium (**the White Vote**): A vote for the leadership of the Coven; it must be unanimous. The White Vote should only be called if a Conclave member feels that the Regis is not leading the Coven properly. It has been called in America only three times: in Plymouth, after Roanoke, when John Carver attempted to unseat Myles Standish; in New York, after the Silver Blood was called to the Repository, and Lawrence van Alen replaced Charles Force; and by Forsyth Llewellyn, after Paris, where Mimi Force prevented a unanimous vote.

The Code of the Vampires (the Code, or the Blue Blood Code): A stringent rule of ethics, not unlike the Ten Commandments. The Blue Bloods hope the Code will help bring about their eventual return to Paradise. It states that humans are not to be dominated or toyed with, but to be respected, so that the Blue Bloods will bring light and harmony and peace to this world.

Compulsion: A seed of an idea that can be placed by a vampire using the glom

The Conclave of Elders (the Conclave): The Coven's highest leadership. The Conclave makes decisions for the future of the race.

Conduit: A Blue Blood's human assistant and caretaker who helps him (or her) navigate the human world and keep the Blue Blood existence a secret. A position of exalted servitude, many Conduit families serve their Blue Blood families for hundreds of years as doctors, lawyers, accountants, financiers, and even best friends. Every member of a vampire family is assigned a Conduit at birth, but many have let go of their Conduits in recent years. If a vampire expires, a Conduit is given two choices: work in the Repository, or have his or her memory erased.

The Conspiracy: A subset of the Committee, dedicated to keeping the existence of the Blue Bloods a secret from the Red Bloods by spreading false information and legends. Many of the myths are rooted in truth.

Consummo Alienari: The little known fifth factor of the glom. It allows complete control over another's mind, subsuming the other's will. For Red Bloods it means instant death; for vampires irrevocable paralysis.

Contineo: A spell that holds a ward in place

Corruption: The process by which a Blue Blood becomes a Silver Blood. By marking a Blue Blood vampire with the Sacred Kiss, the Silver Blood poisons the *sangre azul*, turning the Blue Blood into a monster like itself. It is not an immediate transformation however, and the poisoning is dependent on the amount of blood drawn from the victim. The process can be reversed, or stopped with adequate intervention. The Corruption is complete once the infected Blue Blood takes a fellow Blue Blood vampire to Full Consumption, taking another immortal spirit into its own consciousness.

Coven: A group of vampires living in an area and registered with the Blue Blood community (ex: the New York Coven, the European Coven)

Croatan: An ancient name for the Silver Bloods, meaning "Abomination"

Cycle of Expression: What vampires call the length of their lifetimes. After approximately one hundred years, the physical shell expires, leaving only a single drop of blue blood, which will be implanted in a vampire woman when it is time to call up the spirit for another cycle. Between cycles the vampire rests, evolving, until his or her next Expression. The closely monitored cycles are key to the Blue Bloods' continued invisibility to the world.

Dimidium Cognatus: A being who is half human, half vampire. Unlike the other Blue Bloods, this is a new spirit without a past. The only example in current history is Schuyler Van Alen.

Dissipation: Another term for Full Consumption

Dormi: A spell to put someone instantly to sleep

Elder: The title of Elder is given to a Blue Blood who has served the Committee well for many cycles. This title is usually given upon the one hundredth Cycle of Expression.

Emeritus Member: A Conclave member who has retired. Many were called back to duty after the Rio massacre.

Enmortal: Vampires who choose not to rest and keep the same physical shell over many centuries. They are exempt from the reincarnation cycles; they also do not require the proximity of other vampires in order to live. Some Elders are Enmortals, but it requires a special dispensation from the Conclave.

Eversor Lumen **(Light-Destroyer)**: Azrael's sword, which she receives at every bonding to Abbadon. To be used only in direst need, to be kept hidden from foes, and to strike to kill.

Eversor Orbis **(World-Breaker)**: Abbadon's sword, received at every bonding to Azrael. To be used only in direst need, to be kept hidden from foes, and to strike to kill. Unlike the archangels' swords, which are a bright white flame, this sword is dark gray and edged with silver, with terrifying black marks. It looks more like a primitive ax than a sword.

Evolution: The passive resting stage of the vampire's life, while the spirit awaits its next incarnation. The foremost mission of the vampire race is to evolve to a point where God can forgive them and welcome them back into Heaven.

Expulsion: What the vampires call their experience of "death." The expulsion of the spirit from the physical world.

Facio Valiturus Fortis: A blessing meaning, "Be strong and brave"

The Four Hundred: According to the Code of the Vampires, only four hundred vampires from each coven are allowed to express at one time. There was some confusion in *Blue Bloods*: Repository Records #101, which incorrectly stated that there are only Four Hundred vampires in the world. This is wrong and a clerical mistake on the part of overworked Repository scribes.

Four Hundred Ball: Known as the Patrician Ball in the nineteenth century: the vampire-only, multimillion-dollar party of the year. A tradition that reaches back centuries, where new Committee members are presented to Blue Blood society. An event that celebrates status, beauty, power, money, and blood—Blue Blood.

Frango: A counterspell that breaks a ward on a place

Full Consumption: When a human or vampire is drained of all of his or her blood through the Sacred Kiss. To do this to a human is the biggest taboo of the Code of the Vampires; to do it to another vampire is Abomination.

The Gates of Hell: The seven gates forged by the Blue Blood Order of the Seven to secure the Paths of the Dead. They are meant to keep Lucifer and the Silver Blood demons imprisoned in the underworld. Their physical manifestation in the glom appears to be twelve feet wide and forged into the crust of the earth, but the true barrier is the spirit and protection of Michael.

The Glom: The vampires use the word "glom" to describe two things: a direct line of consciousness that can be used for vampires to commune with one another, or to control the minds of other humans or vampires. It also describes the twilight nether-world that vampires can access—an alternative plane in the universe.

There are five factors to the glom: 1) Telepathy, the ability to read minds, 2) Suggestion, the ability to plant a seed of an idea in another mind (it must be done subtly, so the other believes it's his or her own), 3) Compulsion, the ability to issue a direct order to another's mind, 4) Suppression, the ability to overcome the will of another, and 5) *Consummo Alienari*, the little-known fifth factor, allows complete control over another's mind, but is highly dangerous.

Hibernation: A prolonged sleep that vampires enter at the end of a cycle, when they are weary of immortality

Human Familiar: These are the "lovers, friends, and vessels" on whom vampires feed and rely. According to the Code of the Vampires, familiars are never to be abused, and under no circumstances fully drained; they are to be treated with affection and care for the service they provide, as once taken as a familiar, the human will always feel a special bond with the vampire.

Illuminata: The vampire gift of glowing in the dark, which makes them recognizable to one another

Incantation Demonata: The spell to call a Silver Blood

Infractio: "A breaking." Lawrence uses it to describe what he fears has happened in Corcovado.

Inquisitor: The official prosecutor in a Committee investigation

Intersection: A part of the glom where Silver Bloods can enter but never leave. A limbo between worlds, hidden in the tunnels of Lutetia.

Lucifer's Bane (a.k.a. the Rose of Lucifer): A giant emerald necklace that Forsyth Llewellyn gave to Bliss. It is supposedly made of a stone that fell from Lucifer's crown when he fell from Heaven. Also known as the Holy Grail, Bliss wore it continually until the day of Mimi's bonding ceremony to Jack, when she ripped it off, rejecting any more association with her father.

Lutetia: The ancient Gallic city under what is present-day Paris, it was built by Blue Blood Romans as a massive underground network of tunnels. It is also the location of one of the seven Paths of the Dead and a Gate of Hell. The tunnels are like a maze, enchanted against the *animadverto*, where a vampire could be lost forever. The center is under the Eiffel Tower, where all tunnels eventually lead. There are seven corridors radiating from the center, representing the seven ruling houses of the Blue Bloods. When Gemellus moved the Gate of Time, he left an intersection there.

Mark of Lucifer: A five-pointed star on the neck of a vampire who has been Corrupted by a Silver Blood. It looks like a burn or a cattle brand.

Mark of the Archangel: A mark on the wrist of the Uncorrupted archangels, in the shape of a sword piercing clouds, identifying the archangels as children of the Light. It cannot be duplicated or falsified.

Materia Acerbus (**Dark Matter**): That from which the Silver Bloods come. The opposite of the White. Also the name of a book of black spells in the Repository.

Modo Caecus: A blinding spell that makes humans forget what they've seen

Mutatio: The vampire ability to change into the elements of fire, water, or air, including smoke and fog

Mutatus: The shape a vampire shifts into

"Nexi Infideles": "Death to the traitors!" A Blue Blood war cry

Obsido: An obstruction brought about as a ward

Occludo: Closing your mind to external influence in order to resist the glom

The Order of the Seven: The seven guardians of the Gates of Hell, chosen during the Crisis in Rome and composed of the seven original ruling Blue Blood families. The gatekeepers scattered far and wide and are now unknown to one another and the Conclave leadership for their own protection.

Palaver: A conversation between those of different status: angel vs. demon. Bliss demands a palaver of the demon in her dreams.

Passive State: The resting state vampires enter between cycles. Also called Evolution.

Paths of the Dead: The only remaining passageways between Earth and the underworld, they are now secured by the Gates of Hell, forged by the Blue Bloods at Michael's command after the battle in Rome. In the glom they look like paths of molten lava, hissing with steam.

"Phoebus ostend praeeo": "The sun shall show you the way." It is the cryptic message Jordan leaves for the Venators searching for her.

"Propon familiar": "Tell your friends." The Compulsion Mimi uses to get the little slum girl in Rio to tell the Venators of Jordan's whereabouts.

Quadrille: An old-fashioned figure dance at the Four Hundred Ball lead by the Committee members being presented; the teens in the foremost quadrille are chosen because of their family's hierarchy in the Committee.

Regenerative Memory Syndrome: The process during a vampire's Transformation when a Blue Blood's memories of past cycles return; the young vampires feel as if they are actually experiencing the memory again.

Regent: The second-highest ranking member of the Conclave. The Regent is responsible for the Coven when the Regis is unable to fulfill his/her duties. Also, when the Regis is in the passive/hibernation state, a Regent is chosen to lead the community.

Regis: Head of the Coven and the Conclave, the Regis can only be elected unanimously and blessed by the seven Wardens representing the seven ruling houses. The Regis's orders are law.

Regression Therapy: The process in which vampires learn to access past lives and the accumulated knowledge available to them from their vast past-life experiences

The Repository of History: The Committee headquarters and Blue Blood archives, it holds all the knowledge and secrets of their race. Its towering stacks were once located several stories below the Blue Blood–exclusive nightclub Block 122, but after Kingsley called forth a Silver Blood, it was moved to a "corescraper" below Force Tower, miles underground.

The Sacred Language (the Old Tongue): The ancient, heavenly language of the vampires. Latin is the bastardized, awkward Red Blood version of the language, as the sacred language is not Latin, per se, and does not adhere to Latin structure or grammar. Its historical roots trace even beyond Sumarian script or Egyptian hierogylphs. According to the laws of Heaven, every creature on God's earth must obey commands given in this language.

Sanctus Balineum: The ritual cleansing a Blue Blood bride undergoes before her bonding. Surrounded by her bondsmaids and the female Wardens, she dips into an ice pool, a steamy vapor bath, a relaxing harmony pool, and finally a fire pool, all of holy spring water.

Sangre Azul: The blue blood: it is as old as time and a living database of the vampires' immortal consciousness. It contains their wisdom, vast intelligence, and memories.

Sending: A manipulation sent through the glom

Shapeshifters: Vampires able to change their physical shell at will, for example, into another human figure or an animal. Unlike *mutatio*, not every vampire can do this.

Sigul: A telltale mark or signal, as the emblems of each of the seven ruling houses

Silver Bloods: Immortal enemies of the Blue Bloods who have sworn allegiance to Lucifer, the exiled Prince of Heaven. Like the Blue Bloods, they are fallen angels, but refuse to live by the Code of the Vampires. Enslaved instead to a bottomless appetite of greed, sex, and desire, they now hunt the Blue Bloods. They are insane with the legion of memories they hold. Their eyes are crimson with silver pupils. They each have the strength of a thousand vampires.

Solom Bicallis: A one-way path from the underworld, as in Leviathan's prison at Corcovado. Once it is used, it is closed to all.

Stasis: A locked-in state of paralysis that inhibits motion

Subvertio: A spell that unlocks what can not be unlocked, that destroys what can not be destroyed. A white hole of death. Also called the White Darkness, a vacuum of space and time.

Sunset Years: The years between fifteen and twenty-one—the most vulnerable time for vampires, during which their Transformation from human to vampire takes place and their Blue Blood asserts itself as they come into their full powers. This young generation of Blue Bloods does not use this term, as they find it "corny."

The Uncorrupted: Angels who were not cursed and banished by the Almighty, but chose to leave Paradise out of love for their kind. They are Michael and Gabrielle, the most powerful Blue Bloods on Earth.

Velox: The vampire ability of superhuman speed, so fast that they are undetectable, which leads most Red Bloods to think vampires have the ability to be invisible.

Venatio: The practice of memory hunting

Veritas Venator (**Truth Seeker, Truth Teller**): The highest order of the Committee's secret police. Fearless warriors in the fight to keep the Blue Bloods safe from harm and discovery, they are able to decipher dreams and access human and vampire memories.

V.F.E. (Vessel for Evil): What Bliss calls herself when the Visitor takes over. A way for her to laugh when she really wants to cry.

"Vos vadum reverto": The words spoken at a funeral for a vampire who has left this cycle: "We await your glorious return."

Ward: A secure protection placed on a location by incantation

Warden: Title given to senior members of the Committee and the Conclave

The Watcher: The Elder of Elders is an eternal spirit, born with her eyes wide open, in full consciousness of her memories. She holds vigilance against Blue Blood enemies to sound the alarm should Lucifer return to Earth. She can be called up in a cycle to take human form, but if threatened, can switch human shells. She was the one who first discovered the Croatan betrayal in Rome. Able to see the future, she also foresaw the breaking of the bond between Gabrielle and Michael and predicted that Gabrielle's daughter would be the salvation of the Blue Bloods.

White Darkness/White Death: The result of the *subvertio* spell. Leviathan released it into the intersection in Lutetia, creating a time vacuum that possibly swallowed or destroyed Charles Force. Kingsley called it forth to destroy the Gate of Time and one of the Paths of the Dead.

Wisdom Teeth: A vampire's fangs (the Red Bloods took the term from the Blue Bloods). They are not, as the Conspiracy has spread, in the front canines, but actually on the side. With practice, they can be extended and retracted.

Author's Note: I am currently in the process of writing the fifth Blue Bloods book, Misguided Angel, *coming Fall 2010, and thought it would be fun to share the first two chapters.*

MISGUIDED ANGEL

ONE

The Cinque Terre

Schuyler Van Alen walked up the polished brass spiral stairs leading to the upper deck as quickly as she could. Jack Force was standing at the edge of the bow when she caught his eye. She nodded to him, shielding her eyes from the hot Mediterranean sun. *It's done.*

Good, he sent, and went back to setting the anchor. He was sunburned and shaggy, his skin a deep nut brown, his hair the color of flax. Her own dark hair was wild and unkempt from a month of salty sea air. She wore an old shirt of Jack's that had once been white and pristine and was now gray and ragged at the hem. They both displayed that laconic, relaxed air affected

213

by those on perpetual vacation: a lazy, weathered aimlessness that belied their true desperation. A month was long enough. They had to act now. They had to act today.

The muscles on Jack's arms tensed as he tugged on the rope to see if the anchor had found purchase on the ocean floor. No luck. The anchor heaved, so he released the line a few more feet. He raised a finger over his right shoulder, signaling to Schuyler to reverse the port engine. He let the rope go a little farther and tugged at it again, the stout white braids of the anchor line chafing his palm as he pulled it toward him.

From her summers sailing on Nantucket, Schuyler knew that an ordinary man would have used a motor winch to set the seven-hundred-pound anchor; but of course Jack was far from ordinary. He pulled harder, using almost all of his strength, and all eight tons of the Countess's yacht seemed to flex for a moment. This time, the anchor held, wedged into the rocky bottom. Jack relaxed and dropped the rope, and Schuyler moved from the helm to help him twine it around the base of the winch. In the past month they had each found quiet solace these small tasks. It gave them something to do while they plotted their escape.

For while Isabelle of Orleans had welcomed them to the safety of her home, once upon a time, in another lifetime, she had been Lucifer's beloved, Drusilla, sister-wife to the emperor Caligula. True, the Countess had been more than generous toward them; she had blessed them with every comfort—the boat in particular was fully staffed and bountifully stocked. Yet it was becoming clearer each day that the Countess's offer of protection was morphing quickly from asylum to confinement. They were as far from finding the Gate of Promise as they had been when they left New York.

The Countess had given them everything except what they needed most: freedom. Schuyler did not believe that Isabelle, who had been a great friend to Lawrence and Cordelia, and one of the most respected vampire dowagers of European society, was a Silver Blood traitor; but after Forsyth Llewellyn's treachery in New York, anything seemed possible. In any event they couldn't afford to wait and find out if the Countess was planning to keep them prisoners in perpetuity.

Schuyler glanced shyly at Jack. They had been together a month now, but everything was still so new— his touch, his voice, his companionship, the easy feel of his arm around her shoulders. She stood beside him against the rail, and he looped his arm around her neck, pulling her closer so he could plant a quick kiss on the top of her head. She liked those kisses the most, found a deep contentment in the confident way he held her. They belonged to each other now.

Maybe this was what Allegra had meant, Schuyler thought, when she told her daughter to come home and stop fighting, stop fleeing from finding her own happiness. Maybe this was what her mother wanted her to understand.

Jack lowered his arm from her shoulder and she followed his gaze to the small rowboat "the boys" were lowering from the stern onto the choppy water below. They were a jolly duo, two Italians, Drago and Iggy (short for Ignazio), Venators in service to the Countess and for all intents and purposes, their jailors. But Schuyler had come to like them almost as friends. The thought of what she and Jack were about to do set her nerves on edge. They would not get another chance. She marveled at Jack's calm demeanor; she herself could barely keep still, and was bouncing up and down on the balls of her feet in anticipation.

She followed Jack to the edge of the platform. Iggy had tethered the little boat to the yacht, and Drago reached forward to help Schuyler step down. But Jack slipped ahead and brushed Drago aside so he could offer Schuyler his palm instead, ever the gentleman. She held his hand as she climbed over the rail and into the boat. Drago shrugged and steadied the boat as Iggy brought the last of the provisions onto the bow.

Schuyler turned to look closely at the rugged Italian coast for the first time. Ever since they had learned of the Venator's affinity for the Cinque Terre, they had been advocating for this little day trip. The Cinque Terre was a strip of the Italian Riviera populated by a series of five medieval towns. Iggy, with his broad face and fat belly, spoke longingly of his memories of running along the paths at the cliff's edge before coming home to outdoor dinners overlooking sunsets above the bay.

She had never been to this part of Italy and did not know too much about it—but she understood how they could use Iggy's affection for his hometown to their advantage. He had not been able to resist their suggestion to visit, and allowed them a day ashore, off their floating prison. It was the perfect spot for what they had planned, as trails ended in ancient stairs that stretched upward for hundreds of feet. The paths would be abandoned this time of year—tourist season was over as fall brought cold weather to the popular resort towns. The mountain trails would lead them far from the ship.

"You are going to love this place, Jack," Iggy said, rowing vigorously. "You too, *Signorina*," he said. The Italians had a difficult time pronouncing "Schuyler."

Jack grunted, pulling on his oar, and Schuyler tried to affect a festive air. They were supposed to be getting ready to enjoy a picnic. Schuyler noticed Jack brooding, staring at the sea, preparing himself for the day ahead, and she swatted his arm playfully. This was supposed to be a long-awaited respite from their time on the ship, a chance to spend a day exploring.

They were supposed to look like a happy couple with not a care in the world, not like two captives about to execute a prison break.

TWO

The Getaway

Schuyler felt her mood lift as they pulled into the bay at Vernazza. The view could bring a smile to anyone's face, and even Jack brightened. The rock ledges were spectacular, and the houses that clung to them looked as ancient as the stones themselves. They docked the boat, and the foursome hiked up the cliffside toward the trail.

The five towns that formed the Cinque Terre were connected by a series of stony paths—some almost impossible to climb, Iggy explained as they walked past a succession of tiny stucco homes. The Venator was in a jubilant mood, telling them the history of every house they walked past. "And this one, my auntie Clara sold in 1977 to a nice family from Parma; and this right here was where the most beautiful girl in Italy lived (*kissing noise*), but . . . Red Blood lady, you know how they are . . . *picky* . . . oh, and this is where . . ." Iggy called out to farmers they came across as they walked through the backyards and fields, patting animals as they snuck through their pastures. The trail wound back and forth from grassland to homes to the very edge of the sea cliffs. Schuyler watched tiny rocks tumble over the side of the hill as they made their way forward.

Iggy kept the conversation flowing, while Drago nodded and laughed to himself, as if he had taken the tour one time too many and was merely humoring his friend as Iggy's long-winded tales took most of the morning. The climb was hard work, but Schuyler was glad for the chance to stretch her muscles, and she was certain Jack was too. They had spent too much time on the boat, and while they had been allowed to swim in the ocean, it wasn't the same as a good hike in the open air. In a few hours they had worked their way from Vernazza to Corniglia, and then Manarolla. Schuyler noticed that they passed the day without seeing a single car or truck, not a phone line or power cable.

This is it, Jack sent. *Over there.*

Schuyler knew he meant he had judged their distance to be nearly halfway between the two towns. It was time. Schuyler tapped Iggy on the shoulder, and gestured toward a craggy outcropping that hung over the cliffside. "Lunch?" she twinkled.

Iggy smiled. "Of course! In all my exuberance, I forgot to let us stop to eat!"

The spot to which Schuyler had led them was in a peculiar location. The trail stretched out toward a promontory, so that there were cliffs on either side of the narrow path. The two Venators spread one of the Countess's spotless white tablecloths over a grassy plateau between the rough stones, and the four of them crammed in the small space. Schuyler tried not to gaze down as she snuggled up as close to the edge as possible.

Jack sat across from her, gazing over her shoulder at the shoreline below. He kept his eye on the beach as Schuyler helped unpack the basket. She brought out salamis and prosciutto di Parma, finocchiona, mortadella, and air-cured beef. The meat came in long rolls, or cut into small discs wrapped in wax paper. There was a loaf of rosemary cake, along with a brown paper bag full of almond tarts and jam crostata. It was a pity it was all going to go to waste. Drago pulled out several plastic containers filled with Italian cheese: pecorino and fresh burrata wrapped in green asphodel leaves. Schuyler cut into the burrata and took a bite. It was buttery and milky, rivaling the view in splendor.

She caught Jack's eye briefly. *Get ready*, he sent. She continued to smile and eat, even as her stomach clenched. She turned briefly to see what Jack had seen. A small motorboat had pulled up to the beach below. Who would have known a former North African pirate from the Somali coast would prove to be such a reliable contact? Schuyler thought. Even from far above, she could see that he had brought them what they had asked for: one of their fastest speedboats, jerry-rigged with a grossly oversized engine.

Iggy popped open a bottle of Prosecco, and the four of them toasted the sun-drenched coastline with friendly smiles. He lifted his hand in a wide gesture as he gazed down at the midday feast. "Shall we begin?"

That was the moment she had been waiting for. Schuyler sprang into action. She leaned back and appeared to lose her balance for a moment, then bent forward and tossed the full contents of her wineglass into Drago's face. The alcohol stung his eyes and he looked baffled; but before he could react, Iggy slapped him on the back and guffawed heartily, as if Schuyler had made a particularly funny joke.

With Drago momentarily blinded and Iggy's eyes closed in laughter, Jack moved to strike. He slid a shank out from his shirtsleeve and into his palm, flipped it around, and drove the knife deep into Drago's chest, sending the Italian sprawling to the ground, bleeding from the hole in his torso. Schuyler had helped Jack make the blade from one of the deck boards; he had hollowed out the back of a loose stair tread and whittled it against a stone she'd found on a dive. The plank was made from ironwood, and it served as a dangerous and deadly little dagger.

Schuyler rushed for the other Venator, but Iggy was up before she could stand. This they had not counted on. The fat man could *move*. In an instant, he had pulled the shank from his friend's chest to use as a weapon of his own and turned toward Schuyler, the laughter having died from his eyes.

"Jack!" she cried, as the Venator charged. She couldn't move; Iggy had hit her with a stasis spell when he'd recovered the blade, which he was now holding above her chest. In a moment it would pierce her heart—but Jack dove between them and took the full brunt of the blow.

There was no time to scream. She had to get out of the spell, everything was going wrong too quickly. There was no time to even think of Jack or whether he had survived. She wrenched herself forward with every ounce of energy she had, fighting the invisible web that held her. The sensation was like moving in slow motion through a thick ooze, but she found the spell's weak link and broke through. She screamed as she ran toward Jack's seemingly lifeless body.

Iggy was there first, but as he turned Jack over, he did a double take. Jack was unharmed, alive and smiling grimly.

Jack leaped to his feet. "Tsk, tsk, Venator. How could you forget an angel cannot be harmed with a blade of his own making?" He rolled up his sleeves as he faced his adversary. "Why don't you make it easy on yourself?" he said mildly. "I suggest you go back and tell the Countess that we are not a pair of trinkets she can keep in a jewelry box. Go now, and we will leave you unharmed."

For a moment it appeared as if the Venator was about to consider the offer, but Schuyler knew he was too old a soul to take such a cowardly route. The Italian removed a nasty-looking curved blade from his pocket and pounced toward Jack, but suddenly stopped in mid-air. He hung there for second with a funny look on his face, part confusion and part defeat.

"Nice move with the stasis," Jack said, turning to Schuyler.

"Any time," she smiled. She had taken the edges of the spell that had recently paralyzed her and hit the Venator with it.

Jack took it from there, and with a powerful gesture, he threw the fat guard far off the side of the cliff, sending him crashing to the rocks below.

"You got the tank?" he asked, as they scrambled down the cliffside to the pirate boat waiting for them below.

"Of course." She nodded. They had planned their escape well: Jack had driven the yacht's anchor impossibly deep into the rocky ocean bottom, while Schuyler had emptied the yacht's fuel supply while she was below-decks. The night before, they had sabotaged the boat's sails and the radio.

They ran across the beach toward the pirate boat, where their new friend Ghedi was waiting for them. Schuyler had met him during one of their trips to the St.Tropez market, where the former member of the self-styled "Somali Marines" was helping unload a pallet of fresh fish upon the dock. Ghedi missed his days of adventure and jumped at the chance to help the two trapped Americans.

"All yours, bossing," Ghedi smiled, showing a row of gleaming white teeth. He leaped off the starboard side. He would catch a ride back to the market on the ferry.

"Thanks, man," Jack said, taking the wheel. "Check your accounts tomorrow."

The Somali grinned more widely, and Schuyler knew the fun of stealing the boat was almost payment enough.

The massive engine roared to life as they sped away from the shore. Schuyler glanced to where the two Venators were floating, lifeless, in the water. She comforted herself with the knowledge that both would survive; they were ancient creatures, and no cliffside fall could truly harm them. Only their egos would be bruised. Still, they wouldn't be able to recover for a while, and by then she and Jack would be well on their way.

She exhaled. Finally. On to Florence, to begin the search for the keepers and secure the Gate before the Silver Bloods found it. They were back on track.

"All right?" Jack asked, guiding the ship with expert

ease through the stormy waves. He reached for her hand and squeezed it tightly.

She held it against her cheek, loving the feel of his rough calluses against her skin. They had done it. They were together. Safe. Free. Then she froze. "Jack, behind us."

"I know. I hear the engines," he said, without even bothering to look over his shoulder.

Schuyler stared at the horizon, where three dark shapes had appeared. Their forms grew larger and larger as the crafts drew closer. Apparently Iggy and Drago hadn't been their only jailers.

Escape was going to be harder than they thought.

ACKNOWLEDGMENTS

Many thanks and love to the people who helped bring this book to the world, especially my husband and collaborator, Mike Johnston; my editors, Jennifer Besser and Christian Trimmer, and the rest of the super-fabulous team at Hyperion; my agent, Richard Abate; Kathryn Williams, for her helpful research. Thank you to the DLC, Green, Johnston, Torre, Ong, and Gaisano families. Thank you to my readers. Love to all!